CLASH OF STAR-KINGS

Wildside Press Books
by Avram Davidson

Clash of Star-Kings
The Enemy of My Enemy
Island Under the Earth
Joyleg (with Ward Moore)
The Kar-Chee Reign / Rogue Dragon
Marco Polo and the Sleeping Beauty (with Grania Davis)
Masters of the Maze
Peregrine: Primus
Peregrine: Secundus
Rork!
Ursus of Ultima Thule

CLASH OF STAR-KINGS

by Avram Davidson

WILDSIDE PRESS
BERKELEY HEIGHTS • NEW JERSEY

CLASH OF STAR-KINGS

In this book, the author has taken some liberties with the geography of Mexico, but none (he trusts) which may not be forgiven a sincere friend of that great nation.

First Wildside Press edition: April 2000.

The increase of population and prosperity in and around that great and ancient habitation, the City of Mexico, has brought with it a great many innovations, ranging from the brilliant new Museum of National Antiquities and Patrimonial Treasures to very unbrilliant smog. The visitor who has enjoyed the riches of the former and finds, if he is fortunate, his view of the outside world unimpeded by the latter, can look up and away—very far, indeed, away—and observe the snowcapped outlines of two great and sacred mountains: the splendid shining cone of Popocatepetl and the magnificent snowy sierra of Ixtaccihuatl. The latter, the "white woman" (thus, the meaning in the Nahua language of these syllables, so all but insurmountable to the Anglo-Saxon tongue), was believed by the Aztecs to be the bride of the sun; and, indeed, bears an uncanny resemblance to a figure of a reclining woman: head, bosom, body, hands and feet, all covered in white. Her companion, "smoking mountain," was set there to guard her.

Little guard was needed to keep away the Indians, whose religious awe alone restrained them—as it did, until too late, from resisting the Spaniards. Cortez, thinking in terms of a different universe, knew a volcano when and where he saw one, sent his lieutenant, Diego de Ordaz, with nine men, to make the ascent. They ravaged the sacred and burning mountain and descended with enough sulfur to make gunpowder. The snows of Ixtaccihuatl remained unsullied. The record does not say if the sulfur was wrapped in fennel stalks like the stolen fire of Prometheus, or if eagles tore at the liver of the audacious Iberian. Probably not.

In the confrontation of the conquistadores with the civilizations of Mexico and Peru we have a situation almost Science Fictional: the potent monarchs submitting in scarcely comprehending resignation, and all their millions of subjects, to the handfuls of men who might well have come from another planet—so alien were their weapons, their manners, and their minds. It is ironic that the Dukes of Montezuma, descendants of the Aztec Blood Royal, became and are, still, grandees of Spain. There are moments, and not a few of them, when the Conquest seems never to have taken place; when one sees the Indians emerging from their brushwood huts, huaraches on their feet, serapes of ancient pattern wrapped about their bodies, drinking the immemorial *chocolatl* from tiny earthen pots. . . .

But then the antique and pre-Columbian silence is broken by the roar of the jet plane, and the elder design reveals, once again, that it has cracked into fragments of an almost infinite number. Standing on the threshold of space and all which that implies, it is well to be reflective.

The town of Los Remedios does not attract tourists in any great numbers; indeed, it has few amenities to tempt them. Sitting as it does so high up on the slopes of *los volcanes* and surrounded by forests, it has very pure air—and very thin, too; a heart unaccustomed to altitude tends to pump hard and tire easily. There are few famous antiquities, no night clubs, no swimming pools, and its tiny hotel, though clean, has not even running water.

A second-class bus service runs several times a day, requiring several transfers between the town and "Mexico" ("City" being understood), and a cheerful Toonerville trolley of a narrow-gage railroad known as the *mas o menos* because it comes chugging and smoking and whistling to and from the junction at Amecameca twice a day—*"more or less."* The roads are never in good shape and the weather is usually cold, with frequent rain and often mist.

Now and then a party of alpinists comes through en route to assay the heights of Popo and Ixta, as the mountains are familiarly known locally; or an archaeologist appears to examine the mysterious Tlaloc in the cave; and of course a considerable number of outsiders appear for the feria of El Heremito del Monte Sagrado. There is one Lebanese merchant, called *el Turco*, one Syrian corn-buyer, called *el Arabe*, a refugee Austrian misanthrope, *el Alemán*, and three citizens of the U.S.A., called —with a shade more geographical accuracy than the inhabitants are accustomed to—*los norte-americanos*. These constitute the only inhabitants of the district who are not in whole or in part of Indian blood.

They also constituted the only inhabitants of the district not, at the moment, seemingly totally preoccupied with the approaching fiesta. Not only had extra and ramshackle buses been laid on to transport the visiting pilgrims, but retired engineer Juanantonio Calderon Cruz—whose boast was that he had once transported Zapata—had come out of retirement to navigate a special train—by the appearance of locomotive and rolling-stock, the same one. There were a great many cars and trucks (though few new ones), a great many horses and mules and burros and crude wagons—and a great many dusty feet. There was even a platoon of cavalry from the Federal District. The marketplace was like an anthill and the top of Monte Sagrado (where now stood the 17th-century stone church which replaced the 16th-century adobe one, which had replaced the original Aztec pryamid) was like another, with the roads and paths in between like ant trails.

Every hour or so another procession started up the winding trail with its banner, usually of either the Virgin of Guadalupe or the Virgin of Los Remedios (slightly less popular, she was suspected of anti-Republic sentiments), pausing meticulously to make pagan offerings to the sacred *ahuehuete* trees which lined the way. But all these were but opening acts before the day's main event: the procession down from Monte Sagrado and all through the town and then back of the figure of the sainted Heremito. Everyone was anticipating this with great pleasure—with the probable exception of Sarah Clay, the pleasantly plump and sometimes charming wife of Jacob Clay, one of the two male Northamericans of the town.

Sarah, at the moment, had fixed her soft pink mouth into a discontented line and was breathing noisily through her small and freckled nose. The source of her annoyance, Lupita, the Clays' maid, stood before her in the patio making dramatic faces and gestures. She was small and scrawny and squinting and walked with a curious shuffle and was not a very efficient maid, but maids in Los Remedios—good or bad—were hard to get. "Infirm," she was repeating now for the twentieth time, speaking rapidly and mixing in many words of Nahuatl. "Infirm—in bed—mother—alone—mañana—infirm—"

The mere sight of the beautiful Douanier Rosseau patio denuded of almost all its flowers and branches by the landlady, Señora Mariana, to make decorations for the fiesta, had put Sarah in a bad mood. Plus the fact that Evans, the tootsie cat, for whom Sarah had saved a dinner tidbit, was nowhere to be seen. And now this. *This*, being Lupita's intention of absquatulating and the need for Sarah to speak Spanish. "He did not will know why your (plural) mother so often was also infirm," Sarah said. "Why

not used to could procure a doctor to was meeting
her, and return?''

"Infirm!" cried Lupita, seizing the word, trium-
phantly. "Malady very malign! Immediate atten-
dance!" She rolled her eyes up, hideously, arched
her back, and twitched vigorously to indicate the
malignant nature of her mother's malady—adding,
encouragingly, "But mañana will be better!"

"Oh, all *right!*" cried Sarah, who didn't believe a
word of it, Lupita bugging out so often on account of
maladies unknown to science and holy days of obli-
gation unknown to the church. Adding, too late,
"But by favor to wash the utensils since?"

Lupita, already halfway to the gate, half-turned
her head. "Mañana, Señora! Mañana!"

Sarah thrust out her lower lip. Unless the dishes
were washed for supper the Clays would have to sup
off market-bought prepared foods, and their bud-
get showed a cash-on-hand status of only five pesos.
She recollected the tidbit in her hand for the tootsie
cat, so cunning with his markings like a black and
white bunny. "Evans!" she called. "Evans. . . ."
Her voice became disconsolate, her lips more prom-
inent. "Oh, well," she said, after a moment,
"maybe he's only gone off to shack up with the
convent cat." She smiled a trifle. Then she saw the
pile of dirty dishes, the scuttlebutt of icy cold water,
and the fiber scouring-pad; and her lip went all the
way out and she began to snuffle.

Lupita went shuffling along at a rapid pace down the
rain-rutted street. The plaza of Los Remedios had

once been paved in preparation for the expected visit
of Maximilian, but nothing else had ever been paved
before or since. Avoiding the principal avenues and
streets, aflutter with women and children and even a
number of men preparing the decorations and altars
for the forthcoming procession, she made her way by
a series of knight's moves to the outskirts of town—
very abruptly demarcated here on this side by a deep
arroyo. Into this she slid rather than climbed, and
passed beneath the shadow of her own house, from
which the sounds of groaning and grinding indicated
that her mother—an aged, blind crone—was preparing tortillas. Lupita did not look up, but she did look
back. So. Bautist was there coming along behind.
Good. And there, up ahead—Solita. The others were
probably already there.

And there, after a long uphill trudge which took
her and her two companions alongside ruined walls
and across little rivers and through groves of trees
and around cornfields—but always away from
houses and always uphill—there at last she found
them: Ruiz and Dolores and Gustavo. Gustavo had
hold of a rope on the other end of which frisked a
very young, black goat-kid. Lupita broke off a pine
branch and swept the ground, Dolores sprinkled it
with water from a gourd, Gustavo and Ruiz began
the saying of that which needed to be said. Solita
built a tiny fire on which they all sprinkled copal-
gum and, while one of them waved a turkey wing to
spread the fragrant smoke, the others thrust scraps of
cloth and hair combings and bits of colored corn
dough into the crevices of the ancient tree. Then Ruiz

took a sharp pair of scissors and cut the kid's throat and, while the others sipped the blood collected in the calabash and sprinkled it around and on each other, Ruiz took up the razor-sharp piece of black volcano glass and cut out the animal's heart and they offered this at the base of the tree and they all bowed down.

Then Gustavo hid the carcass where it would be safe and on top of it they hid their clothes and they dressed in the coyote skins which had been there and they smoked themselves in the odorous embers of the fire and then urinated on it and painted designs on each other's faces with the paste of ashes. Then they started off—up, up, always up—twitching their rumps from time to time so that their tails wagged and now and then they went a short way on all fours and now and then they chanted and now and then they howled.

"Josefa, the Widow of Gomez," as she signed her name on the very few occasions which ever arose for signing it, had gone out to gather herbs in the woods and uplands which stretched away so endlessly and sloping until they came to the dead region of black volcanic sand which surrounded Popo or the gaunt escarpments of the base of Ixta. Señora Josefa had a great devotion to the Blessed Crown, to which she had commended herself before starting out on her little expedition, and it was beyond doubt this which had preserved her from death or even worse. The late Señor Gomez had been of a mature age at the time of his marriage, and his death had left the widow with no more than a good name, a small *granja* in the country and a small *quinta* in the town: plus two children. So Señora Josefa had gotten out the black garments which she had worn after the death of her first husband, rented both properties as best she might, reserving the greater part of the income for the education of her son in "Mexico," and moved with her daughter into the house of her sister, Mariana, the Widow of Matteos. The possibility that she might offer, or her sister accept, money for room or board had never occurred to either of them. By her needle, which was skilled, she was able to supply young Marinita with clothes; and as for other expenses—gifts, for example, or masses—these she supplied by gathering and preparing and selling herbs.

On this occasion she had in mind particularly to gather a great basketful of the tender leaves of the *cedron* tree, which, decocted into a tea, are excellent not only for the kidneys of older men but also for various feminine periodic infirmities which are not the affair of men of any age. She also wanted to find, if possible, some poppies and yellow daisies and violets, all of which make good preparations to wash the bodies of those afflicted with weaknesses and fears. These were her specific needs for the moment. Naturally she kept her keen eyes open for anything else which Providence might place in her path, such as roots and buds and barks useful in cases of irritations of the body, or mushrooms . . . half of which might be exchanged for butter enough to fry the other half.

Although she felt the trip to be necessary—
otherwise she would not now be engaged upon it
when she had much rather be back preparing decorations for the procession—and although she had made
it hundreds of times before, Señora Josefa felt a
measure of nonspecific uneasiness. For one thing,
there were soldiers in town, and although the manners of soldiery had improved since the troubled days
of the Revolution, still, well, soldiers. . . . Then
there was talk about the Tlaloc; Señora Josefa was
not worried about the Tlaloc, not in the least, she was
a good Christian and her opinion about the Tlaloc
was that he should be left totally undisturbed where
and as he was. As for the mysterious lights said to
have been seen on and around Popo, she did not
doubt but that they were made by sulfur poachers,
that was all, there was nothing more to it, and she
wished they would go away. As for other things,
there were no other things which could justify her
feelings. Nothing major. But many things minor.
And yet—

What difference did it make if some woman whose
figure she had seen for years without noticing, or
noticed for years without seeing, should suddenly lift
her head and look Señora Josefa in the face boldly
and almost threateningly?—she realizing, with a
sort of shock, that she had never seen the woman's
face even once turned to her before. It meant nothing. Still . . . still, there was a certain change of
atmosphere, subtle and intermittent, and it had
bothered her. Well. Of nothing. To the work, without dawdling or dallying, then back in time to make

the Stations of the Cross on Monte Sagrado and visit
the Holy Hermit before he was carried through the
town on his annual peregrination. She fell to, her
strong fingers nimbly stripping the twigs of the desired leaves.

If one had asked her the meaning of the offerings
hung upon the *ahuehuete* trees between the Stations,
she would have answered, mildly and gravely
amused: "Things of the Indians, Señor—of nothing." And if one had asked her what or whom she
meant by Indians, her answer would have been,
"Poor people, Señor, who cannot afford proper
clothing." And, consequently, when she saw what
she saw, and her fingers grew frozen and still, she
was neither perplexed nor confused: merely hor-
rified.

Señora Mariana de Matteos was as short and round as
her sister Josefa was tall and slender, but her thicker
fingers moved, nonetheless, deftly now as they had
been moving all day long . . . not alone in the usual
tasks of the house, but in preparing for the feria or
fiesta. Let no one be able to say that the Quinta de
Matteos did not prepare itself properly for the passage of the procession of the Holy Hermit! Nimbly
and skillfully those fingers had prepared chains and
garlands of cunningly twisted colored "china" paper, had prepared and set up archways and banners
and legends, had stripped the garden of both the front
patio where she and her sister lived and the back
patio where the Señores Clay lived, of almost all
flowers and greenery. The petals had been plucked

and dropped into baskets according to color and
Señora Josefa had just finished sifting the last of
them into a series of flower-petal pictures and patterns in the road in front of her house. She always did
so. But none of them, she considered, as she regret-
fully turned her eyes away—equally ready to scowl
if any passerby showed signs of walking in the road
or to beam at any praise—none of them had ever
done better than this. It was when she saw that the
feet heedlessly trampling the floral designs belonged
to her sister Josefa, that she realized something must
be dreadfully wrong. She seized her arm and hurried
her into the patio.

"Sister, what passes?"

"Oh, woe of me! Sister, what have I seen!"

'My God, Sister, what *passes?* What *have* you
seen?"

Josefa dropped her basket, and fled into the tiny
room which housed the family altar, pausing only to
utter the single and scarifying word, *"Naguales!"*
before falling on her knees before the huge framed
picture of the two Virgins and the flickering votive
lamps, and, crossing herself with her beads, began to
pray aloud with sobs and tears and shuddering
breaths. Mariana lifted her trembling hand to her
gaping mouth, swayed, then, with heavy steps, followed her sister and knelt beside her. It was a while
before she had recovered enough to think of anything
beside prayers.

Finally the two of them went in the kitchen and, at
the table, Josefa sipped a drop of ancient Spanish
brandy bought during Señor Gomez's last illness,
and then sipped a cup of very potent black coffee.

Mariana asked the inevitable question: "How do you know that they were *Naguales*?"

Josefa threw up her hands and rolled her eyes. "How do I know? First, I heard them. I said, 'Coyotes here and in the daytime?' Then I saw them, loping along, and I felt my heart grow weak, for whoever saw six coyotes one behind the other in a straight line? And then—*Cristo Milagroso!*—they rose to their feet and went upright and beneath the skins of the coyotes they had the arms and legs of men!"

Mariana crossed herself. "*Jesus-Maria! Jesus-Maria!*"

"So I knew that they were neither coyotes nor men, but Naguales. Sister—woe of me! Sorcerers and were-coyotes! *Brujas* and *brujos*, witches and warlocks! God alone knows what troubles and evils will come upon us now that they dare to show themselves again in the open!"

The sisters each took hold of one of the other's hands and, as with their free hands they crossed themselves repeatedly, they chanted:

> "*May we not die of fright,*
> *May we not die without confession,*
> *May that fright fall into the ocean,*
> *May those that cause that fright fall into the*
> *   mountains,*
> *May it seize only the wicked and the infidel and*
> *   the malevolent!*"

They gazed at one another in silence a moment. Already they were beginning to feel somewhat bet-

ter, and a righteous and determined anger was beginning to replace the fear in their faces. "So," said
Señora Mariana, grimly, "they are up to their old
tricks once more, are they? Worshippers of evil
demons! And to pick this day! Oh, the malevolent
ones! Oh, how the Naguales hate the Holy Hermit
and his blessed catafalque! Oh, how they hate the
priests! Aren't the witches always trying to destroy
the good Hermit?—and who knows that they might
not have harmed him more than once if he did not
trick them by slipping away in the night and vanishing off to Rome to serve mass there before daybreak!
Well!" She rose to her feet and seized her scissors.
"I'm not going to rest a minute, I'm cutting rue and
rosemary, both so good against witches—and *cor-
dones de San Francisco*: may it bind them hand and
foot! And even the little rosebuds, like drops of
blood from the Sacred Heart—we will dip them all in
holy water and place them all around. . . ." She
paused a second at the doorway and looked back at
her sister. "For Heaven's sake, Josefa," she cried,
"don't just sit there doing nothing: *Pray!*"

It was quite different keeping house in the United
States, Sarah thought, for the manyeth time. There it
was all so simple. There was hot and cold running
water, O-cello sponge mops, detergents, Comet
Cleanser, Campbell's Soup . . . all the conveni-
ences of modern science. *Here* there was nothing but
a barrel of water so cold that it burned like fire and a
sort of concrete sink without a pipe (there *was* a pipe,

elsewhere in the patio, but it lacked a sink) and a fiber pad. You had to dip the dirty dish all greasy cold into the ice-cold water and scrub it with the pad and your fingers froze and then you put the dish, which looked no cleaner at all, in the sink and dipped some more melted snow out of the barrel and poured it out and it ran and splashed all over your legs— "*Ow!*" screamed Sarah. "OW—OW!" The dish slipped and shattered.

Sarah swore. If it weren't for the few bits of flowers and herbiage still left in the patio she would have wept. . . .

No use telling Jacob. Not him. That stinker. That bastard. Would he offer to light a fire and try to make hot water, let alone once *help* her? No. He wouldn't. Not him. She knew his rotten, selfish moods . . . just let her put her head in the door of his workroom and *tell* him about mean, selfish, ungrateful Lupita and he would, without doubt, *yell* at her! As though it were *her* fault they had only five pesos left and he had to meet a deadline with the damned story he was working on. *He* wouldn't care that tootsie little Evans had run away or been catnapped or something! And here she had thought Mexico was going to be such a *fun* thing, all loyal smiling hardworking native servant girls and lovely tropical beaches like Puerto Vallarte in that picture with Liz Taylor. Tropical! Here she stood, risking frostbite and only a few sprigs of herbs and a few stalks of little purple flowers and one bush with tiny-tiny rosebuds on it—

At which, in stomped Señora Mariana and, with-

out so much as *looking* at Sarah, began to cut all the
rest of the green stuff and the flowers! The grease
congealed, Sarah's fingers got stiffer and redder and
colder. "All right for *you*, Richard Burton!" She
wept. . . .

Luis Lorenzo Santangel knew well the networks of
little paths which led through the woods and rocks
above even the highest pastures, led eventually to the
small *milpas* where grew the life-sustaining corn of
the Moxtomí Indians, who raised no cattle, not even
so much as a goat. Milk, they held—and it seemed
logical—was for infants; and if it came ever to pass
that the small brown *tetas* of a Moxtomí mother had
no milk for her infant, why, there was always the
milky pulque, good for young and old alike. And, if
despite this benevolent liquor made from the fer-
mented nectar of the maguey cactus the infant
died, why, how sad—only not very sad—it was
destinado that the tiny soul become a tiny angel in
Heaven.

The townspeople were, as a matter of course,
scornful towards the Moxtomí, calling them
cerrados—closed ones—because their minds were
closed to all things modern and innovating. They
laughed at the Moxtomí, so meek and so mild, at

their bare feet and naked legs and blue-black serapes, their ignorance of proper Castilian speech and at their poverty and pagan ways. Townspeople had, over the course of centuries, alienated the greater part of the Moxtomí *ejido*, the communal tribal lands: no wonder the Moxtomí were so poor! Had the church done anything to prevent this? No. Small wonder, then, that these poor, good Indios were more than half pagan.

Most of all, perhaps, the townspeople scorned the Moxtomí because of their dark Indian skins, unlightened by a single drop of Spanish blood.

This was not the least of the reasons why Luis felt himself to be so close to these Indians and considered them his friends. Why—it was not a week ago that Don Eliseo, the unlicensed veterinarian, come to inject the cows of Luis's father, had asked, "Is this your oldest son?" And Francisco Santangel had answered, grudgingly, hastily, "Yes. . . . But you can tell that he doesn't take after *my* side of the family because he is so dark." He always spoke like that of his son . . . his own son. And it was true that Luis was the darkest child of the family. He was the best behaved child at home, and the least favored. He was the brightest student at school, and the most neglected. Fathers and mothers did not favor him as a suitor for their daughters unless the daughters in question were themselves too dark or too poor or too old or ugly or of too ruinous a reputation to hope for a suitor of lighter complexion. Luis, nevertheless, had finished school and, moreover, had even taught himself English—and what might he hope for in the way of a career?

He might hope for the crumbs of the table, the jobs left over after the fairer applicants had been placed—regardless of their other qualifications in comparison to Luis. This was the ineradicable stain in the Mexican garment, the fatal inheritance of the Conquistadores and their Conquest, and he hated it. He even hated "La Conquistadora," the Virgin de los Remedios, because she had come over with Cortez's men and remained the patroness of the Spaniards. Other "true" Mexicans, dark as or darker than Luis, even though they might be less acutely sensitive, would tend to favor the Virgin of Guadalupe, who had no European origins, who had appeared shortly after the Conquest to the humble Indian convert Juan Diego: others might. Not Luis. He didn't speak of it, but in his heart, deeply, he hated the Roman Catholic Church as much as he hated the Spaniards and his family.

For a while more he would still try to swim upstream and ignore the snubs. There was a faint possibility that he might be able, nonetheless, to make his way successfully in the modern world. And yet— still if he failed—what then? Would he be content to live as a failure in the world which had refused him success? No. No, never. Rather than that, he would defy them all and shame them forever. He would do what no one of Christian education and secular, modern training, of even partly Spanish blood, had ever done: leave this corrupt civilization behind for-

ever. Burn his modern clothes. And put on the home-
spun and the blue-black serape of the Moxtomí, ask
for a dark-skinned daughter of the pueblo and an
allotment of the shrunken *ejido* land. Already he
knew much of the Moxtomí language; he would
perfect his knowledge; they would initiate him into
the sacred secrets which the townsmen did not know
and, indeed, scarcely knew existed. And he would
dance the holy dances and perform the sacred
ceremonies and sing the chants to the Great Old
Ones. . . .

Only not yet.

His heart had begun to beat faster at the prospect,
as it had used to at the prospect of a woman before he
had ever really had one. But the joy of making a
woman part of himself was a transient joy and this
other anticipated pleasure would be a permanent joy.
And so he hesitated. For, with every delight there is a
sorrow, and the delightsome life of the Moxtomí
Indians had a very sorrowful side, indeed. Almost
every bit of it had its roots in poverty and this poverty
was due entirely to the loss of the greater part of the
ejido lands. He told himself that he might not do it,
after all. . . . But underneath the thin meniscus of
confidence in his ability to prosper as a modern man
was a deep certainty, part pleasure and part pain, that
his future lay not in an office or an apartment but in
the small huts of the Indians, warm only in love and
history.

There was, of course, never any doubt in his mind
that the Indians in question were the Moxtomí. The
Tenocha Indians were infinitely the more numerous,

incomparably the more powerful, and there was even a vigorous movement among them to give official status to their language, the Nahua dialect, which they called *Meshika*. The fact that Luis knew very well that his maternal grandmother had been a Moxtomí did not blind him to the probable fact that the blood of the Tenocha flowed in his veins as well as a heritage on both familial sides. But who and what, after all, were the Tenocha? Who else but the Aztecs! And were they not themselves the seed of a pre-Spanish Conquest? They were themselves aliens here on the upper slopes of the great valley. The Moxtomí, the last and furthest-flung of the Toltecs—it was to them that this land rightfully belonged.

And all the while Luis's feet led him up through the stone-strewn and balsam-scented paths.

But his mind was elsewhere and on a multitude of things.

He wasn't going up to El Pueblo de San Juan Bautista Moxtomí merely to enjoy the friendly presence of such acquaintances as, say, Tío Santiago Tuc, or Domingo Deuh, who was more of Luis's own age. There were *things* he wanted to discuss with them, a variety of exciting things, and he wanted their opinions. There, up ahead, a huddle of brown brushwood and adobe, he saw the pueblo. It was still a good way off. Luis began to form his thoughts into mental conversation.

"There are soldiers in town, Uncle Santiago, soldiers from 'Mexico' with horses and rifles. Why, do you suppose? I don't really think that this time they've come to expel any Indios from Indio lands; their business seems to lie only in Los Remedios *municipalidad*. But there's a further question, you see—*what* business? It has to do with Monte Sagrado, I'm sure . . . everyone is sure of that. Some say that they're here to keep order at the feria of the Holy Hermit. Some say there's going to be, I don't know, some kind of trouble with the procession. You know that not everyone in town is the *Heremito's* friend—particularly not in the *Barrio Occidental*—that's a mean, tough neighborhood; you know that. Today I heard a saying I haven't heard in a long time: *Scratch a Nahua and you find a Nagual.* . . . What do you think that really means?

"And others are saying, Tío Santi, that the soldiers are here for another reason altogether. They say that the government is going to take away the Tlaloc that's in the cave under the Monte and take it to 'Mexico'—I don't know why. And there's talk that this would be a bad thing, that if they do this the Tlaloc will be angry and that there will never be any rain again in the whole Valley. Some are angry about this and some are just excited and of course some don't care at all."

The turn in the path at this point brought Luis face to face with a view which might alone make the fortune of a hotelier. To his left the great Valley of Mexico sloped downward like a precious bowl, and he could see the farms and fields below the rim of forest. Very far below him, and seeming quite small, was his native hateful town of Los Remedios, a huddle of red-tiled roofs at the foot of Monte

Sagrado—so high it seemed from down there—yet from here a mere hummock, apparent only because crowned with the church. More fields, more forests, dwindling, dwindling . . . a tiny wisp of smoke: the *mas o menos* steam locomotive panting its way uphill from Amecameca. And, to the left of the misty huddle which was Amecameca, from here the land fell away abruptly into another valley and another state and another and altogether different climate. To Luis's right the land rose unmarked by man except by the meager *milpitas* of the Moxtomí, rivulets and gorges and woods and great riven boulders: the Pass of Cortes like a line of demarcation between the gigantic sleeping woman in her white shroud which was Ixtaccihuatl and the looming cone of glistening ice-clad Popocatepetl.

Luis gazed and sighed and resumed his walk and his cerebral conversation. "Domingo Deuh, my friend, have you and your people seen the lights which are said to have been shining and moving about on *los volcanes?* I myself think that I have, once or twice, but I am not entirely sure—perhaps they were stars peeping out from behind clouds, or *aeroplanes* passing high and silently between the mountains and myself. Still, many others and some of them sober and serious witnesses have claimed to have seen them, and in such a manner that neither stars nor *aeroplanes* could account for them. Do you know anything of this? Have your people formed an opinion?

"And what of the smokes from Popo? Mountain-climbers have come down with reports of such. Did they lie? Were they mistaken? Has the long-slumbering Smoking Mountain begun to stir again? Or have interlopers descended to dynamite the sulfur inside the crater and carry it away to sell without having to pay taxes on it? And are these smokes only from their blasting, or from fires started, by their thievery?''

Ahead, dogs began to bark. Luis selected a stout stick, advanced the short remaining way, running over in his mind his concluding sentences. "Are none of these reports true, my friends of the Mox-tomí? I would like to speak to you about them, and you to speak of them to me . . . keeping in mind what you have told me, that there is a meaning to be gained from falsehood, as well as from truth—''

The lean and hungry dogs of the hamlet came hurtling and howling at him; he flourished his stick, stooped and rose, making the gesture of throwing a stone at them. "*Sucsé!*" he cried. "*Cuidado!*" They retreated, still glaring at him with shining, hungry eyes, but still leapt up and down and barked frenziedly—much more so than usual. He wondered at this—

But not when he saw the uproar in the hamlet itself. The people, usually so quiet and sedate (though never of course so subdued up here as when down below in the lands where Castellano was spoken), were gathered in the open, waving their arms and all but shouting at each other, now and then leaving one group to walk rapidly—or even run!—to another. Luis stopped stock-still for a moment, astonished; then walked on, hailing them. His first syllables were almost drowned out in the hubbub; his final ones fell upon so absolute a silence that they faltered and stopped.

They whirled around and looked at him, and he could see the shutters falling behind their eyes, the masks sliding down over their faces. He did not seem to see anyone precisely walk off, the gathering seemed to sink away, somehow, to be absorbed into the houses and alleys and as ants from a disturbed area will appear to melt away into the clods of the field. And, by the time he had walked over to Tío Santiago Tuc and Domingo Deuh, who awaited him gravely and sedately . . . and totally expressionlessly. . . . no other man or woman was beside them. This so disturbed him and his thoughts that he was long in speaking again, and all the while the black eyes in the brown faces (one smooth and young, the other graven and old) looked into an invisible hole between his eyes and through it and out beyond again.

He had come for nothing; this was clear, certain. He might just as well have been the tax collector, for all that any trace of confidence was visible. But he would not give up: it was more than that he wanted to discuss specifics, he would (he felt) *oblige* them to remember and to restore the atmosphere of that especial relationship which had previously been between them. He knew it would be useless to ask them, directly, why they were agitated before he arrived and why they were now behaving to him as they were. So he began to speak as had been in his mind to, all the long way up, in hopes that not only might he get meaningful answers, but that, in the course of conversation, the stiffness between them would melt away and the former easiness return.

Soldiers in town: why? *How would we know, Señor?*

Trouble with the procession? *Up here, we hear nothing.*

Take away the Tlaloc? *Oh . . . Ah . . . Mmmm . . . (sigh) . . .*

Lights on the volcanoes? *We are ignorant Indios . . .*

Smoke on Popo? *Popo? Smoke? We see nothing.*

And a silence fell, and Luis, overcome with disappointment, slumped . . . winced . . . sighed. Suddenly, a small, a very small sign of a smile appeared on the face of old Tío Santi. He patted Luis on the shoulder, took him by the arm, urged him along, did not even let him look back to see if Domingo Deuh was following. Luis relaxed into a wonderful feeling of relief . . . more than relief . . . of happiness. It had all been merely a test! And he had, somehow, *¿quien sabe?* passed it: and now the old man was about to reveal everything to him. . . . It had been a shock, though!

The two of them stooped and entered a hut and sat down on their haunches. Old Tuc said something in Moxtomí, patted Luis again on the shoulder, and left the hut. And the two old women and the very young girl bestirred themselves. He peered about, allowing his eyes to accustom themselves to the darkness, saw only the ordinary accoutrements of a poor Indian household, and a number of sober-faced babies, and waited for the old man to return.

"Long walk . . . . you," the older old woman said, speaking in a deliberately debased Moxtomí, as though he were incapable of understanding anything better.

He said, in his best command of the language, "Has Tata Santiago very far to go before he returns?"

"Yes, very far—you. Tired. Hungry. Eat—eat," she said, as though not understanding, and gave him tortillas with beans and a bit of chili. The other old woman poured him some stale pulque. And the girl began to roast a handful of squash seeds over the tiny charcoal fire. It was not until he had dutifully cracked the last of these that it occurred, belatedly, to Luis, that old Tuc was not coming back at all! And he ceased, suddenly, to be the bewildered friend of the humble and dispossessed autochthones and became, totally, the outraged Mexican male upon whom an insult disparaging his *machismo*—his maleness—has been put.

Bad enough that he, having come with warmth, should be greeted with coldness! Bad enough that his sincere inquiries had been repulsed with assumed ignorance and feigned indifference. Worse, he had been tricked! But worst of all, he had been given over to the custody and the ministrations of women, two old hags and a child, as though he were no more of a man than the infants on the earthen floor! It was not to be tolerated! Rage choked him—they did not think

he was a man, then? Not worthy of masculine cour-
tesy? So—he would show them if he were *macho* or
hembra! He half-rose from where he was sitting. . . .

But the sudden ugly flame, which sprang more
from outrage than from lust, died down quickly. The
women were too old, dry and shriveled like mushrooms, and the girl was far too young—it would be
like mounting a boy. . . . Besides, this was their
village, they would certainly make a commotion,
and Luis might indeed cease very suddenly to be very
much *macho* at all after the men were finished with
him.

He muttered a Moxtomí thanks and farewell
which almost choked him, and walked off with stiff
and angry strides away from the cold and meager
hamlet and its empty streets.

With distance, however, came reflection; with
reflection, forgiveness. Why should they have
trusted him? What, after all, did they know of him?
His overtures of friendship might, for ought they
knew, have been false. Wasn't his father a landowner? If he, Luis, were a Moxtomí, with a memory
of loss of tribal communal lands which had gone on
over the course of over four centuries, it might very
well seem cause for suspicion. . . . Only— Why,
now? Why had suspicion of his intentions (if such it
was) never manifested itself before? Or, at least,
never in this form? What had suddenly upset them
. . . for they had, he now clearly recalled, been
upset *before* he arrived. The source of their mistrust
of him must therefore lie in something apart from

him . . . and, almost certainly, in something apart from *them*. . . .

What could this be?

He had no doubt that it lay, somehow, in the very matters he had desired to question them about; which he, in fact, *had* questioned them about. And since they would, and perhaps really could, tell him nothing, it thus behooved him to find out the answers himself and then *tell them*. His imagination began to soar once again, and, looking down from mental heights upon a landscape only partly imaginary, saw things it had been accustomed to see before. But now it saw clearly in detail as well as in outline things of which it had previously seen as only semi-concealed hints. He saw these so clearly and so richly that it no longer was possible for him to doubt them. In his disappointments with the modern world ruled by *guerros* and *blancos* of "purer" Spanish blood than he, in his sullen retreat from it, he had failed to appreciate that his knowledge of it could make it possible for him to use it for his own (and his friends') ends—and thus totally to defeat it. Would this be *machismo* or not?

Thus and therefore . . .

He would not only find out the answers to the mysterious questions which must be not merely puzzling but vexing the Moxtomí—and thus gain their full friendship and confidence—he would do more than that; he would solve, somehow, (details did not concern him now) the basic Moxtomí question of all: how to regain the lost *ejido* lands, and by regaining them transform the Moxtomí from the huddled handful they now were to the prosperous people they had once been, and—with the help of Luis Lorenzo Santangel—would be once again.

The sun on its way down seemed to turn the edges of the Valley into gold.

III

Robert Macauley, a stocky, self-contained sort of man with shrewd blue eyes and a large blond mustache, was the connection which had brought the Clays to Los Remedios . . . via the *Concerning the Author* note attached to a story of Macauley's in a little magazine they happened to come across. Jacob had liked the story well enough, more than he had any of the others, which was less praise than it merited, but it was the words *"now lives in Los Remedios, a small town in the State of Mexico"* which had hooked their attention. They had moved, freshly married, from New York City, a place which Sarah declared contained no oxygen, to the Currier and Ives community of Pickering, Pennsylvania, wherein they had learned, by and by, a number of important things, such as that: it had, and for good reason, a suicide rate higher than Sweden or Japan; two can't live as cheaply as one; their landlady, a virago with a face like a malevolent horse—ah, well. . . .

"If we can't make more money, then let's go where the money we can make will go further," they said. And they said, "If we've got to move, let's move far away in one jump." And they said, almost in one breath: " *'Los Remedios, a small town in the State of Mexico'* —hey!" They wrote immediately to Macauley and received a fairly immediate reply containing the magic words, "My own expenses amount to about $50 a month," and beat it the hell out of Pickering, Pa., one step ahead of litigious Mrs. Moomaw's latest writ. The trip south, via a disintegrating station wagon whose sale to them almost seemed to have been arranged by Mrs. M., standard-gage, auto-bus, and narrow-gage r.r., so exhausted them that they couldn't have moved any farther if Los Remedios had looked like the Pit of Purgatory instead of rather like an Andean village shoved north by a glacial drift. Finding Señora Mariana's back patio house had been, they were not long in realizing, a stroke of luck, for Los Remedios was not much designed for accommodating foreigners.

Another thing they soon picked up was that living there was not going to cost them anything as low as $100 a month, either. Curiosity mingling with annoyance, Sarah said, "Mac, how do you manage to live here on only $50 a month?"

"I sleep with my landlady," he said, very simply.

"Oh. You didn't tell us that."

"If I had, you wouldn't have come, and I wanted some people I could speak English with."

Their expenses ran them something close to $200

a month, but this was still about $400 cheaper than life in Mrs. Moomaw's semi-renovated barn, plus the fact that Señora Mariana would as soon have entered a brothel as a court of law. Besides her truly benevolent assistances, they had six rooms for $20, including a large studio with a skylight where Jacob Clay, a thin, frenetic man enraged by the difference between what he was writing and what he knew he was in theory capable of writing, typed and cursed and periodically poked his head out to see if the mail had come with assignments or checks. At least once a day they went over to Macauley's house and at least once a day he came over to theirs. Another approximately $20 went to Lupita, but by now Lupita had managed to extinguish any guilt feelings either of them had had for paying such wages.

So now, at the moment, while Jacob crouched at his typewriter like an outraged toad, and Sarah sulked her way through the dishes—only not very far through them: the water was *cold*—Macauley sat on the coping of a dry fountain in the patio and talked. He talked of his stories, for one thing, and his fears (in which Jacob, who mildly admired the stories, concurred) that despite their merits they were far too far out of current literary fashion to achieve any notable success. "So I decided to take time off— from the one about the childless aunt who schemes to replace her sister-in-law as Foremost Female Figure in the children's lives . . . by the way, a standard plot item in Mexican soap opera . . . nobody cares about a philandering husband that much—and repair

Lenita's kitchen ceiling. I'd like to put in a fireplace but she wouldn't know what to do with one. The Mexicans have never discovered the chimney, they're moving right from the charcoal brazier to the atomic pile; meanwhile, let the smoke find its way out—that's their attitude. It took me only about half the time that it would have taken a carpenter, but it would have driven a carpenter crazy to watch me!'' he said, with cheerful pride. "Carpenters are always driven mad to see the way that miners work because we always do everything ass-backwards . . . according to them . . . but we get it done better and quicker. Any miner can handle wood, but did you ever see a carpenter who could handle explosives?''

"No," said Sarah, rubbing her rapidly chapping hands. "I didn't know you used to be a miner . . .''

"Once a miner, always a miner. . . . Say, don't forget the procession tonight. You won't want to miss that. It's quite a thing.''

She felt that she would gladly agree to miss every procession that ever was or would be, even if led by Jesus of Nazareth riding a zebra, in exchange for getting the dishes done. But of course nobody would take her up on it. She noticed that young Mexican who spoke the strained English come into the patio. Mac spoke to him in rapid Spanish, the boy asked something about Jacob, and Mac gestured to the study door. Sarah felt too subdued to warn him off, and besides, if Jacob shouted at the boy he might work off all his hostilities and be in a good and sympathetic mood towards her. She sighed heavily and looked glumly at the dishes.

"Tell me about the procession," she said, dully.

"Jacob, you are busy?" Luis asked, entering the long room with its yellow-washed walls and long trestle table laden with piles of books and papers.

Luis, entering, had no more substance or reality to Jacob Clay than, say, the Ghost of Purim Yet to Come. He thought of a sentence he wanted for his next paragraph, and smiled, vaguely. Luis, encouraged by the smile, came in and sat down in the cane-bottomed chair with the red, white, blue and green floral designs. Jacob jotted down the sentence in pencil; it was not quite ready to go through the typewriter. He looked up and gazed abstractedly at Luis in the chair, not altogether noticing either of them.

"I can speak to you in confidence and in Español?" asked Luis. "I may to make the light?"

Jacob muttered, "Sí, sí . . ." without more than barely understanding the question. It was getting on towards dusk. He peered up at the light, scowling. The light went on. Good. He began to reflect on the sentence. Absurd, that he should allow one paragraph to hold up this whole damned piece, but . . . mmm . . . how did it go, now? ahhh . . . *He was not merely overwhelmed by this new calamity, he was   by it* . . . yeah . . . okay . . . mmm . . . so: *He was?* what? *by it*. . . .

"You are very kindly. *Bueno. Entonces, mira, Jacobo*—" Luis began his confidences, haltingly to begin with, but with gradually increasing fluency.

He felt no contradiction in explaining his secret problems to a foreigner; indeed, had Jacob *not* been a foreigner, Luis would never have dreamed of making him a confidant. True, Luis distrusted . . . feared . . . hated those of lighter skins—but only those of lighter skins who were *Mexicans*. It was they, after all, who had snubbed him; not the gringos, to whom all Mexicans were alike. Jacobo was as polite to him as he was to Don Umberto, the Municipal President. Let Don Umberto mutter about the loss of Tejas and Alta California by gringo conquest, gringo theft. How many thousands of hectares of *ejido* lands had not Don Umberto's townsmen acquired that had once been conquered and thefted from the Moxtomí! It was not the Moxtomí, after all, who had lost Tejas and Alta California. Luis was as indifferent to the yanqui conquests there as any African nationalist was to Russian conquests in central or eastern Asia. It was his own losses he resented, not losses in general, and the enemies of his enemies he regarded as his friends.

"*Entiende, Jacobo, ayer en las montañas . . .*" he said, earnestly.

Jacob regarded him, serenely and unseeingly. *He was not only overwhelmed by this new calamity, he was—he was—he was—* Okay, he was what? washed out? flooded out? No . . . no . . . no . . . But something like it. Luis was talking. Luis was asking something. Who knows what. Jacob Clay made a sympathetic noise, continued to search his mind for the *mot juste*.

● ● ●

Robert Macauley smiled a smile of anticipated pleasure and stroked his golden mustache. A chance had
been given him to enlarge on his favorite subject,
The Secret History of Mexico. Usually he liked to
reveal new entries for The Worst Thing That Happened to Mexico ("The worst thing that happened to
Mexico was the expulsion of the Jesuits; literacy
dropped seventy percent in a generation," or "The
worst thing that happened to Mexico was the pub-
lication of the Papal Bull against Freemasonry;
liberalism and religion were divorced forever."),
but Little-Known Insights he cherished almost as
much. Sarah's question was right up his alley.

"'Who was the Holy Hermit of the Sacred Mountain?'" he repeated. "That's a good question. Let's
precede it with another one. 'Why is the Sacred
Mountain sacred?' Hey? I suppose that this town has
been rebuilt a dozen times at least, since the Conquest . . . but I bet that if you traced on a map the
route this procession will be taking you'd have a
pretty good outline of its original boundaries and
axis. Now, obviously, the Sacred Mountain was
sacred when Huitzilopochtli or Quetzalcoatl used to
have the concession. The old Aztec flay-'em-alive
boys had one of their cardiectomy clinics on top of it,
you can be sure of that. It's got an uninterrupted view
of both Popo and Ixta, the Super-Sacred Macro-
Mountains. And, naturally, Cortez and Padre Ol-
medo, his chaplain, didn't waste any time in toppling
the idols and setting up a cross in their place.

"The Indians wailed a bit, but they didn't really
object *too* much. Know why? Know what their big

objection was? That the Spanish cross didn't have equidistant arms! Sure. The natives already *had* the cross as a religious symbol. The old bishops claimed this proved that St. Thomas the Wandering Apostle had stopped off here in Mexico on his way to India. And the Mormons, of course, claim that this proves that Jesus was here, just as Joseph Smith said. But the simple fact of the matter is—and there's other proof connecting this with Monte Sagrado, I'll get to that in a minute—the simple fact of the matter is, that a cross with equidistant arms was the ancient Mexican symbol of the rains which come blowing down bringing blessings from every direction, and all four cardinal points in particular. But still: what made *this* hill with the pyramid holier than any other hill with a pyramid? And particularly after it ceased to have the pyramid?''

"Was there anything else on the hill?'' asked Sarah, beginning to get interested despite herself.

Mac smiled an a-hah sort of smile and raised his eyebrows and his index finger. " 'On' it? *'On'* it?''

"Well, what then? *Under* it?'' she said, at a venture.

Instantly he leveled the index finger at her face. "Exactly. Exactly. How did you know? Who told you? They don't usually care to discuss it with outsiders.''

Sarah beamed and raised her hands, palms out, to the level of her ears, in one of her favorite gestures. "You mean that there *is* something under it? Oh my goodness!'' She uttered a squeal of sheer delight.

"What? Tell me? Hidden treasure?"

"Tlaloc."

"Who? What—what?"

"There's a Tlaloc under, or perhaps I should say, inside, the Holy Mountain. A statue of the rain god. At least, some say there's a whole statue. But all that's visible is the head. I'm not sure there *is* any more than just a head. It's in a sort of tunnel or cave, or—if my miner's experience is my judge—a combination tunnel and cave. How they got it in there beats me, because the way is so narrow you more or less almost have to wiggle on your belly like a reptile—and it's not carved out of any kind of stone that was ever found in, under, there, either.

"Never mind how I got permission, I have certain strings I can pull if I need to," he said, winking, "but it took some doing. The good clergy have done about all they could to christianize the surface of that little mountain, but *nothing* could ever de-paganize that head. Try to imagine it"—he said, glee giving way to sober sincerity—"this gigantic head—must be a good six feet up and down and across—eyes half-closed—broad nose—full lips—expression of infinite majesty and calm—"

"Gee—!"

"—nothing Aztec about it in the world, it must be *pre-*Aztec, Toltec, maybe, or even Olmec. And—get *this*, now: it's situated under a sort of seepage spot from a spring . . . and the impression that you get, when you turn your flashlight on it, is that, well, damn it! That it's sitting under a sort of gentle rain!"

"Gee!"

"Yes, exactly. Well . . . even though hardly anyone has ever seen it, because you've got to go through the church precincts and the priests have got it closed off and shut up with a good ten stout gates with enormous locks, still, everyone knows it is *there*. All of which is background as to what makes the Holy Mountain holy. Now, as for the Hermit himself, well. . . ."

What the Hermit's original name was, Macauley had been unable to learn; he wasn't even sure that it was on record. But it was a matter of history that he had been some sort of pagan priest or attendant at Monte Sagrado when the Spaniards arrived and that he was just about the first to accept baptism. The Spaniards made him a catechist and, Roman Catholic priests being then and for a long while thereafter in short supply, his influence as a catechist was immense. In fact, he might well have become a Roman Catholic priest himself—except that no natives were ordained at that time at all. Weren't trusted not to be relapsable, in short.

But Juan Fernando, as his baptismal name was, nevertheless, had lived a devout religious life, never marrying, showing an excellent example, quietly exhorting and instructing, chastity, poverty and obedience and all that, respect of Spanish and Mexican alike . . . and, when he finally died, was buried right there.

"Right up there?"

"Right up there. . . . Only he didn't stay

buried. He's still on view, in that glass-covered catafalque that they'll bring around tonight. A sort of local example of popular canonization. To the Church, of course, he is no saint. But to the people, he's very much a saint. Oh, a few times, some superscrupulous bishop has decided that this is an illicit cultus and has tried to suppress it. But not for long. The most the priests here will commit themselves to, if you ask them if it's true, as the people say, that the Hermit takes off at night for Rome every now and then and serves the Pope at mass—oh, they'll sort of click their tongues and give a quick shake of the head. . . .

"But . . . you know . . . I'm not sure that they're totally convinced that he *doesn't!*

"And of course there's a lot more. I could talk all night. For instance—I've never been able to find out, to make sure: is that actually the Hermit in the catafalque? Or a wax effigy? Or a waxen covering *over* a mummy or bones? It's all covered with embroidery, except the head and hands, and you can't get close enough to make *sure*. I'd sure like to know. Oh, well—maybe someday I will!"

He smiled. Sarah said, "Gee . . ." Her sense of wonder was very pleasantly excited. And just then a dish slipped out of her slackened hands and crashed into pieces. "More *cachi-bachis!*" Macauley said, pleasantly undisturbed. "Be sure you stick them up in the fork of a tree."

Sarah said, "Damn! Oh—damn it!" And burst into tears.

• • •

*He was not merely overwhelmed by this new catas-
trophe, he was . . .*

*He was not merely overwhelmed by this new catas-
trophe, he was . . .*

"So there you are, Jacobo," Luis wound up.
"Now, please, tell me, honestly, your opinion.
Please." He looked at the face of his confidant. And
the face lit up with sudden insight. Luis's heart
bounded. He leaned forward.

" *'Inundated'!*" Jacob shouted. " *'He was not
merely overwhelmed by this new catastrophe, he
was inundated by it!*' Ha! Ha-ha! Good! Great!" He
leaped to his typewriter and began to attack the keys.
A minute passed, and another and another, with
Jacob uttering little squeaks and grunts. Then he
ripped the papers and carbons from the typewriter.
"There!" he cried. "And stap my vitals if we don't
put it aboard the packet boat to sail at first tide
tomorrow morning!" Then he blinked, smiled
slightly, frowned slightly. "Hello, Luis," he said,
cordially. "Didn't see you come in. . . . What's
new? Anything on your mind? Eh? *¿Que pasa, joven?*"

Amidst much, much excitement and after many false
alarms, the inhabitants of, and visitors to, Calle de la
Independencia were finally outside and awaiting the
approach of the procession. Archways of wire and
flowers and greenery and electric lights spanned the
street at several points and were boasted by a number

of individual houses, as well as banners reading *Bienvenida Heremito*. Down the street, in front of the house of the Rosario family who kept the pulque saloon, an altar had been built, like a small stage, a glorious gallimaufry of gauze, lights, candles, colored cloth and paper, gilt, silvering, angels, crucifixes, images, and Mexican flags. Even Coco, the idiot cow-tender, usually in a state of agricultural grime, was cleanly washed and dressed and wore a brand-new sombrero in his hands. Fireworks sounded, grew nearer. So did a curious medley of musics. Sky rockets hissed and wooshed and shot sizzling upwards and exploded with bangs and bursts of stars, and the procession rounded a corner and came into sight.

All the religious confraternities in town, it seemed, were there, members and banners and huge burning tapers, as well as many from out of town. The women for the most part dressed in white, those who were not in white were all in black, mantillas or rebozas covering their heads . . . except, curiously enough, the women members of the lay religious orders. Their dress was something in between uniform and habit: all bareheaded, as though to emphasize that they were *lay* people and in no way contravening the secular law against the wearing of clerical costume in public. Men, though outnumbered, were numerous, clutching their sombreros; children were present in profusion, and all walked slowly and gravely with their eyes cast down, voices raised in something half-chant and half-hymn. Group after

group, band after band, banner after banner. . . .
Jacob thought, as he did again and again, how, for an
ostentatiously secular republic, Mexico managed to
be so very and so constantly and so demonstrably
religious.

The marchers proceeded on with measured pace,
the voices paused, the music was suddenly heard
again . . . and a very odd music it was, too: the
repetition of a single bar over and over again, of a
kind of music which had certainly never come out of
Spain—odd, archaic, impressive, stirring, baffling.
The musicians came into sight: three Indian men,
one with a flute, one with an odd sort of drum, and
one with something vaguely resembling an
ocarina—

But before he could fully take this in, from down
the street, a rather sad and shabby and tiny "orchestra" in run-down uniforms with run-down in-
struments of the conventional sort, burst into an
off-key version of a tune he recognized (after a
moment) from having heard it in the United States, to
wit, "Good Night, Sweet Jesus"—and the native
players fell silent. And on this note of bathos and
anachronism, the spectators fell to their knees and
the catafalque, borne on the shoulders of a dozen
young men, approached and passed by.

It distantly resembled a sort of truncated four-
poster bed, with frame and canopy of dark and carv-
en wood, with sides of glass. Jacob strained, Sarah
strained, Macauley strained, to see what was inside.
Again the resemblance to a bed . . . someone was
lying down, covered with a profusion of (so it

seemed) embroidered, richly embroidered, bed-
clothes, drawn up to his chin. The face was dark,
very dark, scantily bearded, in total repose, on its
head what seemed to be a skullcap or headdress of
equally rich fabrication. They thought they could see
the hands, too, but the procession did not halt. The
catafalque seemed to float by in a sea of sighs and
candleflame; the rockets hissed and wooshed; the
near-19th-century orchestra reached the end of its
piece; once again the tootling and the beating of
the weird and totally non-European, yet tantaliz-
ingly evocative melody motif, over and over
again. . . .

There was a silence. Those who had knelt now
rose to their feet. The beautiful and elaborate designs
and patterns of flowers had been churned into chaos
by the passing feet. Señora Mariana smiled as she
noted this. Sarah asked, somewhat disappointed, "Is
it all over?"

"*¿Es terminado?*"—Macauley.

"*Sí, ya es terminado, Señores.*"—Señora
Mariana.

"Well, it's all over, folks. I'll be getting home. I
suppose my *chula* landlady has all kinds of goodies
waiting in honor of the fiera. Come around tomorrow
for breakfast, okay?"

Already the streets were emptying. The Clays
proceeded past the kitchen where they saw the two
older women and the girl bustling about laying a
table, opened the door into the back patio and proceeded through the gloom to their own apartment.

"Well, that was interesting," said Jacob, brightly.

"Hey, honey, what's for supper?" Sarah, with a pang of sheer horror, remembered the still-largely-unwashed pile of pots and dishes and cutlery—and the evil barrel of water, icier and freezinger than ever! Fortunately, before she could reply, in bustled young Marinita, prettily aproned, and carrying a neat stack of well-filled dishes. She smiled, she spoke, she lifted a napkin, she withdrew.

Sarah's spirits soared. "Well, isn't *this* nice," she cried. "Our landlady has made holiday goodies, too! Look, look, all kinds of luscious things—two, no three kinds of tamales! and tacos and tostados and enchiladas, and—look! look! Quesadillas, too! Oh, yummy! See how they're made with colored corn-meal, red ones and blue ones and even green ones. Oh—"

Jacob said, "Eat, eat. Later, we'll talk. . . . Don't bother setting the table, let's eat them with our fingers as the Mexicans do."

Sarah said, serenely, entirely forgiving the land-lady for denuding the patio, "Very well, if that's the way you want to do it, that's the way we'll do it. Who needs knives and forks? . . . Yum yum yum yum. . . ." So much for washing in ice water. And tomorrow breakfast at Macauley's. Now—if wicked Lupita would only turn up before lunchtime to-morrow—!

And while most of the people in that part of town through which the procession had already passed were snug and happy in their houses, eating traditional foods and dipping them in special *mole* sauces and washing it all down with lots of pulque, there was still a good stretch of town through which the procession had yet to pass. . . . And this included a rather bad stretch of town, the ward called the *Barrio Occidental*, or Western District. Here were the most tumble-down houses, the filthiest pulquerias, the raggedyest children, the raunchiest whorehouses, the highest proportion of glowering faces and of drunken brawls and slashings. And here a curious sort of ceremony sometimes customarily attended the procession's passage—a dozen or so of the younger men would halt the procession and ask, with truculent politeness, to be allowed the honor of bearing the catafalque through the barrio. The offer was always refused (when it was made, which wasn't always); sometimes there was a bit of shoving and pushing, usually the occidentales were bought off with presents of dulces, cigarettes, feria-foods. But, if so or not so, the procession after a short while continued on its way past the sullen, scowling faces of the neighborhood Indios.

But not tonight. Not quite.

"With permission, carriers—" Permission was not granted.

Almost immediately the women who carried the gifts or bribes in case they be needed sensed that something was not as usual. They hastened forward with their baskets of sweets, tobaccos, snacks . . . only to be knocked down, to see their baskets and contents trampled underfoot in the sudden rush for-

ward upon the catafalque. They screamed, there
were shouts and curses, clubs thudded, knives were
drawn and flashed, the orderly procession dissolved
into a riot. One of the carriers clutched his bloody
arm. The catafalque sagged. It was swept to and fro.
It dipped and it swayed in the dim light here, where
no festive lamps burned and tapers fell or were
burned out. Luis, who had followed, rushed first this
way and that, not knowing what to do.

"The Hermit! Save the Holy Hermit! Asesinos!
Thieves!"

It was very dark now, like a scene from Hell, and
then, in a sudden hellish burst of light caused by the
untimely explosion of all the rockets at once, Luis
saw the catafalque come stumbling, heavily, to the
ground. He cried out. He saw the Hermit fall, he saw
his splendid coverings in the dust, he saw the Hermit
rise and look from side to side—

Total pandemonium now. Glimpses of people
fighting, fainting, screaming, struggling. Glimpses,
totally inexplicable, of figures half-human and half-
coyote—

—darkness again—

—the Hermit, with tottering steps, uncertain at
first, then very quickly, vanished into the blackness.

And Luis, seeing the footsteps which glowed
briefly and phosphorescently as they appeared and
then disappeared, Luis followed after them, after the
swiftly retreating figure of the Holy Hermit.

_IV_

Long and long he followed these evanescent tracks,
like the glistening of snail trails or the fitfully cold
flames of the fireflies, up through the hills into the
cold black night where the cold white stars seemed
peering low upon the land of Earth. Sometimes it
seemed to him that he knew the path he followed and
sometimes he was sure that he did not. Now and then
he heard the howling of coyotes and he shivered less
from the cold than from the recollection of every tale
he'd ever heard about the _Naguales,_ the men-who-
were-coyotes, the-coyotes-who-were-men, and
who, as part of wicked sorcery, were infinitely more
dangerous to men than any real coyotes would or
could ever be.

He pushed these fears aside, not only because fear
was not _macho,_ but because these legends stemmed
from the malevolent Meshika, the Tenocha-Aztec
people, whose decadent descendants lived in the
Barrio Occidental; not from the benevolent Mox-

tomí, the real heritors of the land. If indeed the Hermit of the Holy Mountain had Power or Powers—and, after seeing him rise from the dead, Luis scarcely felt capable of doubting it—then his power ought certainly to protect Luis, who was literally now following in his footsteps. Following in something akin to numbness, something not far from a kind of terror he had never known before, following with feet which stumbled now and then not only from the darkness but from fatigue . . . for had he not made the long, long walk up these same hills earlier in the day and then down again? . . . But, still:

Following.

Now and then he saw below him the huddled handful of lights which was Los Remedios; sometimes, very infrequently, a moving spark which he knew must be an automobile, or, likelier, a truck on one of the roads down on the lower slopes; and once he saw the tiny spurt of flame in the fire-box of the *mas o menos*, toiling to Amecameca with a line of freight cars. And overhead, the deliquescent stars dripped dew and delicate mist upon him.

But for the most part he saw only the shining, fleeting footprints of the Hermit, and he hesitated to plant his own feet upon them to guide his steps before the pallid light faded away forever.

How far ahead the Hermit now was, Luis did not know. A faint notion that the old stories were true and that the Holy man was on his way to Rome took hold of him—but he cast it off. The mood of it stayed

with him, though, with all its intimations. Whatever
the Hermit was, he was not a mere corpse or effigy.
Was *not*. Such did not rise and walk off into the
darkness and the mountains. But in the name of . . .
anything! . . . what *did* rise and walk off—
anywhere!—after having supposedly been dead for
four hundred years?

He had not, surprisingly, formed any answer to
this by the time he reached the pueblo of San Juan
Bautista Moxtomí. He was very tired, stumbling
with stiff and twitching legs, eyes burning; he
needed rest and warmth . . . and answers . . .
answers . . . answers. He saw the men posted along
the path, answered their hail in The Language,
passed by them into the small open area which was
the plaza, and there he saw the people of the pueblo
sitting in a wide circle with faces of awe and joy and
inside the circle burned a fire and the night air was
odorous with copal-incense. The Hermit stood beside the fire and spoke in a clear and vigorous voice,
but antique language and although he was standing
and those whom he addressed were sitting, he and
they were on a level of eye to eye. When Luis saw
these others, saw their massive bodies and massy
limbs, their strong broad noses and strong full lips
and their heavy-lidded eyes with pupils of burning
gold, he recognized who and what they were. And he
fell upon his knees and bowed his brow down into the
cool dust of the ground before the Great Old Ones,
the demigods of the Toltecs and Moxtomí, who had
calmly and benevolently ruled over the land before

the coming of the cruelty and incessant bloodletting of the Aztecs.

And who had now returned. . . .

The Hermit (or he-who-had-been-known-till-now-as-The-Hermit) paused in his speaking. And another voice broke the sudden silence, a voice like a great and deep-toned bell of gold and bronze, saying, in the Moxtomí language, "One moment, you who have so long and so faithfully been the Guardian of the Entrusted Thing; one moment only. . . ." The ground shook slightly with the great and measured tread and huge, beautifully proportioned hands took hold of Luis and lifted him to his feet. Dazed, delighted, stricken still with awe, he gazed into the great golden glowing eyes and heard the great golden voice say, "Younger Brother, what is in your heart?"

Luis heard his heart beating, his ears rang, he drew a shuddering breath. "Great Old Ones. Is it you whose lights have been seen on Popo?"

"It is so. And then?"

"I . . . Ah! There are so many things in my heart to tell you, to ask you . . . I . . ."

The lips of the giant figure parted in a faint smile. 'Not now, Younger Brother. Not yet. Take this—" Something was pressed into his hand. He felt a cord of maguey fiber and something metallic, with an embossed surface. "—take health, take rest, and at another time, Younger Brother, it may be that we may listen . . . and answer."

The disappointment was like the falling away of

ground beneath Luis. All day long he had sped and toiled from place to place, asking only to be listened to. But Santiago Tuc and Domingo Deuh had been too busy to listen to him, Jacobo Clay had been too busy to listen to him, and now the astonishingly returned Great Old Ones were too busy to listen to him! Anguish ate at him like acid—but for a moment only. And then sleep, of the most delectable sort as is usually felt only when one knows that awakening is imminent, sleep now wrapped its arms around him. The circle of serenely joyful Moxtomí about the (he now recognized) sacred fire, the still all-but-totally-mysterious figure of the Hermit/Guardian, the titanic figures of the sapient and potent and benign Great Old Ones, all began with a swift slowness to dissolve into the golden mists; and Luis smiled and Luis slept.

The Clays slept, too, in their Krazy Kat style house in the back patio, with barely a straight line let alone two parallel ones in the whole structure, and each room painted in different bursts-of-color tones: restaurant-pea-green, imitation-soda-pop orange, do-not-leave-within-the-reach-of-children-shoe-polish-purple, whorehouse-madam-red, and so on . . . all, presumably, the work of a previous tenant defined by Señora Mariana only as *El Español*. Why does the roof leak so much, Señora? El Español punctured it vigorously, Señor. Why are the holes in the gas stove burners mostly plugged up, Señora? Because of the unwholesome foods cooked upon it by El Español, Señor. Why does the wall in the third room not meet the ceiling in the corner, thus letting in the wind, Señora? Thus did El Español occupy himself, Señor,—Ai, the malevolent one! But take no concern, Señor, we will make all these reparations, excellently. Ah, good, Señora—and when? Mañana, Señor! Mañana!

It was Sarah who awakened first . . . from a dream in which she sat bound hand and foot in a barrel of ice-cold water while Lupita, laughing fiendishly, broke greasy plates over her head. She considered telling Jacob of this latest evidence of ill will on the part of that mean girl, but decided against it because he might kick her for waking him up. But by the time she was fully awake she realized that he was, too, and listening.

"Jacob, are you awake?"

"No."

"Well, what's that kind of, well, *singing*, then?"

"Weird, isn't it?"

"It sounds exciting and interesting."

"That's what I said. Weird."

They sat up and listened. The sound of the song or chant or whatever it was came to them distantly, rising and falling. For a while it seemed to be coming near, then it began to die away as though going in the opposite direction. "Do you think," Sarah began, "that it sounds like that wonderful little tootsie music we saw in the parade tonight?"

"No. No, it doesn't. Much more weird. Barbaric. But I see what you mean. Hmmm. . . ."

Sarah's mind had meanwhile started on another track. *Tootsie*. Evans. Where was cunning little Evans, the tootsie little cat? "Evans?" she called, hopefully, hoping to hear his answering preep and the sudden scamper of paws and then his leap onto the bed and the thrust of his little head against her hand, demanding to be petted and stroked and scratched. "Ev-ans . . . ?"

"What's *hap*-pened to him?" she asked, her voice faltering.

"I can see it now. There he is, shacked up with the convent cat. And he says, 'Well, time to split, babe. See you.' And she—the convent cat—she says, 'Just one more time, lover-poo?' And he says, 'Well, now that you come to mention it, why not?' "

Sarah snuffled and laughed, said that, well, she *hoped* so. But she could not be reassured. Jacob had inclined his head and even twisted it about and cupped his ear so as to catch the odd and vanishing strains of curious sound. But Sarah continued to fret about the missing Evans. He had *never* been away *this* long. The Mexicans didn't understand about cats. They thought they were just *an*imals. Suppose he were *sick*. Suppose he was lying, *hurt*, somewhere?

"Where are you going? You're getting dressed? Why?"

In a choked voice she answered, "Evans!" He understood immediately, and swung his legs over the side. "Oh well . . . one more bunch of nudniks wandering through this town tonight won't hurt it, I guess. And''—the thought occurred to him in mid-shoe—''maybe while we're looking and paging, we might trace down the troubadors.''

It was cold outside, and Sarah muffled her head up warm into the reboza which she had bought in the Langunilla market their first day in "Mexico." A sense of hopelessness came over her, not knowing where to look, and so she simply followed behind Jacob, who was trying to track down the sound of the archaic chanting which continued to rise and fall upon the shifting wind . . . or so it seemed. And about two or three times in every block she called out, tentatively, distressfully, *"Evans . . . ? Evans . . . ?"* But no answering "preep" came, anymore than they ever seemed on a definite track for the music. And then—

A number of blocks away, barely visible in the light of the exceedingly rare street lamps, which was, moreover, a number of blocks *further* away, a figure slipped around a corner and went shuffling rapidly across the road. Sarah clutched Jacob and gestured. He said, "Huh?" She said, "There—there—Lupita—" and then, recollecting herself and her purpose, raised her voice. "Lupita! Lu-*pi*-ta!" She trotted forward, turned her foot, fell heavily against Jacob. By the time they had recovered their balance, the figure was gone. The street, studded with stones and lined with the usual stone-and-adobe houses with peaked, tiled roofs, some of which (with their massive, though worm-eaten, wooden gates) antedated the original Mexican Revolution, was silent and empty.

"Are you sure it was Lupita? And if so, so what?"

"Yes, yes—Lupita—she knows Evans—find her—find her and ask her!" Ask her precisely what, Sarah was not certain of. Ask her if she'd seen Evans, if she'd heard news of Evans, if she had any idea of where he might have gone. . . .

She and Jacob quickened their pace. They were looking for Lupita; they were looking for Evans; they were looking for the singing and chanting . . . gradually the town fell away behind them . . . and all three quests seemed to be leading them in the same direction.

Wherever that was.

V

The last landmark which they recognized was the tottering archway with its weathered Latin inscription, leaning against the one still-standing and still-sturdy wall of the old ruined convent, and straddling what was once part of the Royal Road . . . and was now no more than one of the back alleyways of town. The Clays had seen it before, but had never gone under it or passed it. Three hundred years of continual traffic—before the route was shortened and redirected by Santa Anna in a rare act of public benefit—three hundred years of iron-shod mules laden down with silver bars en route from the mines to Madrid—three hundred years of lumbering wagons with iron-rimmed wheels—had worn the road down below the level of the surrounding land until it seemed rather like the dry bed of an abandoned canal.

But it had also beaten the surface so hard that even a hundred-odd years of neglect hadn't destroyed it;

so that, while the Clays could not see where they were going they had only to follow their feet in order to go there. And by and by their eyes adjusted to the darkness which, of course, began to appear less dark. When the road eventually "surfaced" it seemed to the two of them that they were moving through a light mist suffusing and diffusing a subdued light the source or nature of which was unknown.

Now and then a line of wall ran parallel to the road or went off at an angle, sometimes a palisade or a grove. The scent of the open night was all about, night-flowering blossoms and the sweet suspiration of the trees, the strong and fresh sweetness of growing corn, and, over everything, the powerful odor of the relaxing soil itself.

From somewhere ahead the sound of chanting began once again, a deeper and faster note. "Where *are* they?" Sarah asked. Turning her head from right to left, she called, "Evans? Ev-ans . . . ?"

"Maybe it's another procession," Jacob suggested. "Or—maybe even the same one. Hey? Maybe that's why we don't catch up with it . . . it's keeping ahead of us. Well . . . they'll have to stop sometime. What—?"

She clutched his arm. "Didn't you *hear* him? *Evans! Evans!*"

After a moment he said, "I think I did hear a cat. . . . But I can't say that I'm sure it's *that* cat. . . ."

Sarah, however, had no doubts. Of course it was

"*that* cat!'' Maybe he was following the procession, too! Thinking that it contained his people—trying to catch up with it/them! She quickened her pace, panting, for they were now going uphill. At just what point they left the old main road behind and branched off onto the increasingly narrower path, Jacob did not notice nor Sarah care. Now and then the luminescent mists seemed to part a moment, they could see fires and other lights up ahead, and even once, bathed in the rays of an invisible moon, they saw the incredible heights of Ixtaccihuatl, the serenely sleeping Woman, shrouded forever in her snowy cowl and mantle.

Sarah stopped, breathing heavily. "I . . . I'm not sure . . . that I can go much further. . . .''

"The air does seem a lot thinner up here. Well . . . you want to turn around and go on back?''

Distress and indecision played upon her face. "Well . . . oh . . . just a little bit further. Now, don't say anything. I . . . want to be able to hear. . . .'' Her sentence faded off into a laboring breath. But he understood: to hear if the cat sounded again. He nodded, they started off again, this time much more slowly. But each wondered, secretly, if the sound of the blood pounding in their ears would not prevent their hearing anything so slight as the plaintive mewing of a distant cat.

Sarah, finally, dragged one foot after another, clutched at Jacob, and leaned against him, her mouth open and her breath now a painful gasping. And with that, the winds drove the mists into their faces, wet

and chill and pallid. The winds drove the sound of
the strange and eerie singing louder than ever to their
ears. The winds parted the mists in front of them: and
quite a ways away across the more-or-less level land
where they now stood, unable to go on, Jacob and
Sarah saw a circle of fires burning . . . evidently fed
with some quickly combustible fuel, the thin dry
fallen twigs of the pine or piñole perhaps, for here at
one point one would die down to a glow and there at
another point one would leap up and flare as some
stooping figure replenished it. There were two
groups involved, one inside the incomplete circle
formed by the individual fires, and one outside. This
latter band was nearer to them, more quickly recog-
nizable, but not very much less puzzling for any of
that.

The first, hasty, and not a little frightening impression which they had was that those inside were
seeking refuge from the coyotes outside the circle. . . . Coyotes circling around and around and
back and forth, coyotes suddenly howling . . . coyotes. . . . But even before the matter of distance
and perspective adjusted itself they both realized that
coyotes would not be doing a to-the-rear-*run* ma-
neuver whereby each turned and reversed direction
and all did so at once, now loping clockwise and now
of a sudden loping widdershins. And they realized,
too, that coyotes do not chant, and certainly do not
chant *words*, not even in a totally unfamiliar language. . . .

They were prepared, then, for the moment when

the "coyotes" suddenly reared up and revealed themselves to be human figures clad (or partly clad) in coyote skins. Still, it was marvelous—and eerie, frightening—the way that in stooping and even erect there still remained something so sinuous and animal-like in all their movements. . . .

That was what was outside the fiery circle.

Inside, was something else altogether.

The darkness of night, the slant and diluted rays of moonlight, the flickering-flaring-spurting-blazing-dazzling-dying of the firelight: none of this was designed to help give any clear picture of what was there . . . and the exertion of climbing in the rarified air now tended to obscure their vision from within their eyes. . . . There was a first impression of flashing colors and of odd, misshapen design—as though great grotesque birds had been dressed up by a gifted, but insane, child and set to hopping about in agony upon a great, hot griddle—but, of course, there was no fire within the circle of fire, as there is said to be no wind within the eye of a hurricane. The things moved and jerked about and flashed with gold and brilliant plumes and iridescent ornaments, great grotesque and asymmetrical bifurcated and trifur-cated blunted muzzles out-thrust and huge eyes glaring like gigantic burning coals—

"Oh, I don't like this," Sarah whispered.

He said, "Sh. . . ."

The things within the circle took up the chant in deep and discordant voices distorted by their masks and danced and jerked and moved about. The coyote skins flapped, naked human flesh gleaming as though oiled. Only the smoke of the wood fires, mixing in with the mist, seemed normal or natural. And then smoke and mist closed in once more and the sound fell low once more.

Jacob muttered, "Let's go—"

"Evans—"

"Let's *go!*"

She obeyed, yielded to his commanding arm. He could hear her subdued weeping.

Afterwards, he said, "Look, I know that you're worried about the kittykat, but that was no time and no place to break in and say, *Dispenseme, yo busco mi bicho-gato. . . .*"

"I know," she said, with a snuffle.

"Boy! Are the natives ever restless tonight!"

They didn't say anything more for a very long time, and by the time they came again to the tottering old archway it was already daylight, though still misty. And here they paused. That is to say, Sarah stopped, and as she had been using Jacob as a sort of staff or crutch, he perforce stopped, too. "Whatsmatter?" he grunted.

"So are we going home now?" she asked, in a pity-me-for-surely-you-can-suggest-a-better-notion tone of voice.

"Not necessarily. . . . We can go to the Los Remedios-Hilton, if you prefer? What kind of a question is that? Where else would we go?"

In a teeny-tiny voice she said, "I thought we might go to Mac's house. . . ."

"At this hour?" But a look at her woebegone and teary face stopped his sarcasm. "Well . . . he did invite us for breakfast . . . but even for breakfast it's darned early. What say we go home awhile and rest up?—*then* we can go to Mac's house. Okay?"

But she, in a voice which was almost inaudible, said that she didn't want to go home . . . because it was full of dirty dishes at home . . . And so he, knowing that her stubbornness was often in inverse proportion to the reasonableness of her request, and that if balked she was perfectly capable of simply sitting down under the archway until she took root, he said, "Let's go to Mac's. . . ."

Fortunately, the menage at Mac's also included an aged aunt who retired and rose with the poultry; Tía Epifania had just returned from the *molina de nix-tamal* with fresh-ground lime-boiled cornmeal for the breakfast tortillas, and greeted them as though it was the most natural thing in the world for anybody to be up and around at that hour. "Pass, Yourselves!" she cried, cheerily. "This is Your House!"

Some question as to the house's ownership evidently troubled her niece, however, from behind whose bedroom door a sleepy and puzzled "*¿Quien?*" proceeded.

"*Los paisanos de Roberto,*" shrilled the ancient, and blew on an ember. The niece-landlady, after an astonished invocation to the Virgin of Guadalupe (whom she addressed, companionably, as "Sweety!"), dug Roberto in the ribs with an audible thud. He broke off in mid-snore, and presently appeared, rather rumpled and sleepy-looking, but as amiable as usual. He looked at Sarah's face and blinked.

"Let me perform some quick hydraulics," he said, "and I'll be at your entire disposal." He did and was. Then, tapped and drained and washed and combed, he sat down and lit a brown-paper cigarette and began to talk of some light and humorous matter until he thought that they were sufficiently relaxed for him to ask if anything was the matter.

Jacob hesitated. "Well . . . we had a rather curious experience last night. Or, early this morning, to be more exact . . . maybe . . . I'm not sure of the exact time." And he proceeded, with help from Sarah, to tell what had happened. The account took a while; Mac nodded and nodded, lighting a second Negrita from the first before they were finished.

Then he laughed. "Well, if there were such a thing as a local chamber of commerce, they'd have printed leaflets which I'm sure would have taken a load off your mind . . . if you'd read them in advance."

"What do you mean?"

He shrugged. "Simply that it's customary to dress up in costume at this time of year. The hills around here have got more old customs and costumes and dances and fiestas and fieras of one sort and another than just about any area of comparable size in the country. You just happened to stumble across one of them without realizing it, that's all."

Jacob, though somewhat relieved, was still

somewhat dubious. "Dress up like the old Aztec
gods, too, you mean?"

Macauley shrugged again and smiled again.
"Well, I hadn't heard of that particular one. Or of the
coyote skin one, either. But, Lord! I don't know all
of them, there are so many. About the only one
which is well-publicized is the one that's attached to
the Holy Hermit . . . and that one, of course, even
though it's technically theologically irregular, well,
still, it *is* attached to the church. But most of these
others are purely pagan. Which is to say that for the
whole length of time of the Spanish rule, they were at
least in theory illegal. And hence tended to be clan-
destine. Then when the Roman Catholic Church was
disestablished and some measure, some varying
measure of governmental anti-religious pressure
came along, varying from disapproval and ridicule
down to outright persecution—why, a lot of the
pagan cults and ceremonies got it in the neck, too. It
didn't make much difference to them if they were
suppressed in the name of Catholicism or of
Freemasonry—which reminds me"—he chuck-
led—"no, I'll mention that later. Anyway, so
they went right on being underground, so to say.

"Nowadays very few of them have got anything to
fear, actually, from the law. But, well, these things
are looked upon as silly things which only ignorant
Indians engage in. And even ignorant Indians don't
want to be laughed at, mocked. So they go right on
going off into the woods, you see. Sometimes whole
families sort of split up over it. Say that one family

has a son in the secondary school, well, they know he's bound to be too modern to strip down to a loincloth and dance around, say, a post with home-made hootchemacallits pinned onto it. So the after-noon before the thing is due his father may slip him a few pesos and say, 'Why don't you go visit your cousin in Amecameca—tell him we'd like to come, but we can't get away.' Then, with the kid out of the way, they can troop out to the boondocks and carry on the way Grandpa used to do.

"That's all there is to it, really. . . ."

Jacob was weakening, but was still not convinced. "This wasn't any mere poor-Injun bare-assing around," he said. "Why, those costumes must have cost a fortune! Besides . . . besides . . . I don't know just how to put it without sounding corny and pulp-fictionary—but—well, damn it! Yes! There was an atmosphere of evil about whatever was going on back up there last night! I had the definite feeling that if I'd let on that I was there I might have wound up a patient in what you called the Aztec Cardiec-tomy Clinic! Really, Mac, no kidding around: that was very bad medicine there."

He was about to enlarge on it, seeing that Macauley was at last becoming at least a little bit impressed that this was no mere rustic frolic—but then Lenita appeared. She had so thoroughly re-pented of her earlier brusqueness that she clearly neither remembered it nor desired it to be remem-bered—a plump, dark woman of general good nature and not a single word of English. She bustled Sarah away from the two men with an oh-you-poor-thing manner, reclaiming her for the Improved Benevolent Order of Women—local branch consisting of Lenita, Aunt Epifania, and now, of course, Sarah—and impressed her into service at the business corner of the kitchen. Sarah, as soon as she saw that (a) she was not merely allowed, but encouraged, to take samples of the sundry goodies, and (b) that there were no dirty dishes to be washed, no, not a one, Sarah abandoned the discussion without a pang. She even fell spontaneously into Spanish. "What quality of article will we you were to have making thereunto?" she inquired cheerfully.

Macauley's smile slipped a bit, with her gone. In a lower voice, he said, "Well, there may have been some intended bad medicine brewing around here. Some of the aborigines are really upset, you know."

"Yes, that I gather. But *why?*"

"Government doings."

"Meaning . . . ?"

"Meaning: Tlaloc."

The familiar-unfamiliar word made Jacob frown. Then he remembered. "Tlaloc. Wasn't he the old Mexican rain god?" More than this, the name conveyed nothing to him, because he had been in his studio trying to finish an assignment the while that Rob Macauley had been telling Sarah all about the image in the cave (and/or tunnel) under the Sacred Mountain. But Macauley didn't mind, and he gave his account all over again. Jacob was impressed.

"Sounds as nice as what we saw last night was

nasty. . . . But how are they connected?''

Over the cheerful clatter of mixing bowls Mac said, ''I don't know for sure that they are connected. I just think that they may be. Have you seen the cavalry troop in town? No? Guess you must not have been out of the house yesterday at all, then. Well, it seems to be a fact that the government has decided to remove the Tlaloc to the big new Museum of . . . what's the whole handle? . . . mmm . . . The Museum of National Antiquities and Patrimonial Treasures (how's that for grandiloquence?—not that they haven't got a lot to be grandiloquent about!) . . . yes. . . . Down in 'Mexico.' So the cavalry is sort of here as an advance guard to stake out the scene until the moving men arrive.

''The C.O. is a figure in the classical style, tall and leathery and trim mustache, you know. Colonel Benito Alvarez Diaz, and mind your manners, too. I didn't know why they were here, and I said to him, jovially—why not?—'Ah, *coronel*, are you here for the feria?' Wow! Hey? Guess what hit the fan? I got a fierce little, quick little, stiff little lecture on the fact that the United Mexican States constitute a secular republic. Emphasis: *secular*. And that, in addition, he, *Coronel* Benito Alvarez Diaz, is an educated man and a freemason and—I'm quoting—and that as educated man and a freemason he does not fear and indeed, defies all superstition, whether Christian or pagan! Hey?''

''Well may you say, 'Hey.' ''

Macauley said more. He said that he thought that the army unit was there to give notice that the gov-

ernment intended to stand for no nonsense, either
from good churchmen lay or religious who might not
like any poking around in the Monte Sagrado, or
from good (or, as the case might be) bad pagans who
might and probably would in one way or another
object to the removal of a Tlaloc which had been
there, so to speak, forever.

"But it won't do them any good. Lopez Matteos
wants it down there in 'Mexico' where the tourists
can see it and the antiquarians study it, and you can
bet your ass that's where it's going to go. To wit,
Mexico. And the poor dumb bastards in the boondocks can dance all they want to and complain that if
it's moved there won't be any rain again. . . . It
won't do them a bit of good. I just hope," he added,
"that those poor dumbos, some of whom, mind you,
are my (ha ha) best friends, don't engage in any
transference of hostilities. . . ." His manner was
thoughtful.

"What do you mean?"

A shrug. "Oh. . . . Anybody who isn't from
right around here is a foreigner. You're a foreigner,
President Lopez Matteos is a foreigner, every savant
or non-savant who's ever come here to look at Tlaloc
is a foreigner, and, of course, needless to say that
Colonel Diaz who's here to start taking away precious potent sacred rainiferous Tlaloc is a foreigner.
In other words, to a mind very untutored, which is
most minds, all foreigners are linked together in an
evil intent—hey?—and design. So—"

"*A la mesa, a la mesa, hombre,*" Lenita di-
rected. "Here are tortillas and refried beans for those

who eat the Lord God's food, here is *dulce* of quince
and fresh honey, coffee cooked in the aluminum
maquinita, pure butter of cows, and here is also—
look, look—¡*que linda!*—los pancakes norteamericanos which Roberto has so successfully taught me
how to make—''

Sarah, beaming, licking her fingers, said to Jacob,
''Isn't it *good?* Doesn't it smell yummy? What is she
saying, the tootsie?''

Jacob held out his cup for coffee and his plate for
pancakes. ''She's quoting from the Popol Vuh. It
means, 'Eat, eat; later we'll talk.' ''

Later, however, they were too full to talk. And it
was even later that they finally and leisurely returned
home, full and contented and quite at ease, entering
through the same back door to the back patio they
had left by, and found Evans lying on their doorstep,
stiff and bloody and with his heart torn out and
missing.

VI

The front and back patios alike contained a profusion
of flowers and fruit and nut trees (there was also an
adobe chicken coop, the inhabitants of which tended
to vanish away on the eves of feast days), but there
was also a multitude of such herbs as lent themselves
to domestic cultivation; and these Señora Josefa
picked and dried and sometimes distilled, as part of
her craft and trade. She gave away as much as she
sold and had a fair-sized following among the poor,
who referred to her as *la doctora;* often as not there
were several of them sitting on the bench in the front
patio waiting for advice and supply, neither of which
would cost them a *centavo.*

This morning, however, the bench was deserted
except for a middle-aged and unkempt-looking
woman who kept clutching her knee and groaning.
As Señora Josefa and Mariana knew very well that
she suffered from nothing more than a hangover and
a general (and very un-Mexican) disinclination
either to work or to wash, and as they were otherwise

73

engaged, she was allowed to go on sitting for the
moment. The sisters were in the kitchen going about
their work and discussing this and that with their
neighbor, Señora Carmela, who was poor but honor-
able, in low voices.

"And your tenants?" inquired La Carmela.

"They know nothing," said Sra. Mariana.

"She has appeared disturbed, the fat pretty
one. . . ."

"Yes, because her small cat-beast has not been
encountered."

"How sad," said Carmela, adding, "if there were
four or five children, there would be no time to be
disturbed over cat-beasts."

Sra. Mariana sighed. "They stay up half the night
reading books."

"There is still the other half of the night," La
Carmela pointed out.

But Sra. Mariana was not to be diverted.

"It would be a disgrace for us all to have this
matter exposed before the eyes of foreigners," Sra.
Mariana said, heavily. "Woe of me . . . it seems
like a bad dream. . . ."

" 'Life is a dream and the dream is but a dream
itself. Everything passes, everything passes, but he
who has God lacks nothing,' " quoted Sra. Josefa.
Carmela was crossing herself when they heard the
screams in the back patio.

The shortest way there, in theory at least, was out
of the kitchen by way of the dining room and thence
into the sewing room and then by way of the

storeroom onto a small piazza from which two steps descended onto the back patio. But their passage, accompanied by cries of dismay and assurance, was impeded by the presence in the storeroom of an assortment of items such as sacks of corn kernels for nixtamal and corncobs for fuel, bales of wool and a stack of sheepskins—the screams continued—they about-faced, running out of the storeroom, through the sewing room, into Señora Mariana's bedroom, and, via the dining room and hall, out into the front patio (where the sole "patient" was listening with ears, eyes, and open mouth) and thence to the metal gate which separated it from the back one. Unfortunately, it was not only closed but stuck—this required that it be seized by main force and lifted up about two inches so as to clear the bottom sill. . . . Unfortunately, also, this had to be done quite carefully in order to avoid lifting it up about two and a quarter inches—which would bring it in contact with the electric wiring whose insulation had rubbed off in one or two places—the screams from the back patio were joined by screams from the front one—

The "patient," who had enjoyed it all tremendously, arose and carefully pushed the gate well shut again with a piece of wood. It clicked. She grinned a satisfied, snaggle-toothed grin. She considered a moment, her disheveled head cocked to one side. Then she tiptoed into the kitchen and filled one of the cups on the table from the coffeepot on the stove, added plenty of sugar—*white* sugar, not the stuff scraped from the coarse and sticky brown loaf of

piloncillo—thrust some little cakes and some tortillas into her gaping bodice—gulped down the coffee and tiptoed out again. She decided not to bother
waiting for anyone to return. Her hangover seemed
quite cured. Coffee and white sugar . . . she made a
mental note of that.

It was much nicer than herbs, too.

"Poor little Evans!" said Sarah, through her sobs.
"He never hurt anyone."

"Terrible, terrible!" cried Sra. Josefa.

"What barbarity!" exclaimed her sister. They
hugged Sarah and caressed her and patted her
cheeks. "Poor little beast . . . *no tiene cuidado,
Señora*—you can inter the poor little one over
there in front of the rose bushes. Won't that be
pretty? Oh, poor *señora!* Oh, what a shocking
thing!"

And Jacob pointed out to her that the nature of the
injury meant that Evans had died suddenly and therefore without pain. He got a shovel and dug a tiny
grave in front of the denuded rose bushes, wrapped
the little mangled body in two splendid new ban-
danas of scarlet and gold, and so the interment was
accomplished. Señora Josefa then took Sarah to a
remote corner of the patio where, behind the molder-
ing ruins of the very last *diligencia* to ply the local
roads, one small shrub forgotten in the previous
day's excitement offered sprays of tiny blue blossoms. And while Sarah, still weeping, cut flowers
for Evans's grave, Jacob knocked the earth from the

shovel and said, bluntly, to his landlady, "Who did it and why?"

"Ah, Señor! Last night . . . how shall I explain it to you . . . last night there was a big fight among the drunken Indios in that bad *Barrio Occidental*. They tried to obtain the Holy Hermit, *ai de mi!*—possibly with the intention of holding an oratory service in their little chapel there, although the Lord God knows how they have always neglected it since the days of Don Porfirio Diaz until it is falling apart. But at any rate, there was a big fight: sacrilege—simple sacrilege! And it was long before the Hermit was recovered, pray God that the Sainted One be not angry with us for not having taken better care—but without doubt this barbaric mutilation was done by those hoodlums in a state of intoxication. It is a disgrace for our *municipalidad*. I shall complain upon your behalf to the authorities, Señor, to guarantee that it will never happen again."

Her concern and indignation was obviously genuine. Jacob decided not to tell her of what he and his wife had seen during the night, there on the lower slopes of Ixta. "Many thanks for your offer to make such representations on our behalves, Señora. When do you intend to do so?"

"*No tiene cuidado, Señor. Mañana, Señor. ¡Mañana!*"

But at least Lupita came back.

Sarah, who had been trying a spiritual exercise of determining that she would see in her mind's eye

only the image of the little heap of blue flowers and
not the one of— Sarah was distracted by the sound of
running water in the patio. She went to see . . . and
saw Lupita washing the dishes. Most of the resentment melted in this infinitely welcome sight. Poor
uneducated and downtrodden Lupita, washing
greasy dishes so humbly and uncomplainingly in
ice-cold water!

"*Buenos días, Señora.*"

"*Buenos días*, Lupita. I to hope where your
mother was much improvised in their infirmity?"

"Ah, yes, *alabada sea Dios*. The most of the
malignness is terminated. Thanks."

"Of no one." Now that the dishes were clean, it
was time to think about making lunch. But Sarah
didn't want to think about making lunch. Making
lunch was a grunch. People shouldn't have to think
about such things when they were griefstricken. Of
course, the fact that they were griefstricken didn't
mean that they weren't *hungry*. People could be
griefstricken and hungry at the same time. That was a
well-known fact. "I am not sensing myself well
today, Lupita. Dost thou-plural thinking of to could
tamales prepare whatsoever?"

"Excellently. How you will taste! Preparing tamales of green chile, tamales of chicken fat, milled
meat, and of *mole chocolado*. One little moment,
terminating the utensils."

"Oh, yummy!" said Sarah, clapping her hands.
And went to tell Jacob, who had returned from mail-
ing his manuscript. He agreed it did indeed sound

yummy. He went to his studio and stared awhile at
the pale yellow walls and the lithograph of Maximilian in its cracked frame. Lupita's head passed by,
en route with the rest of her to get water for the
nixtamal dough. He tapped on the window. She
squinted, smiled, came to the door.

"Did I not hear singing last night, Lupita?"

"Securely, Señor. There was much singing. The
feria, you know."

"Ah, yes. The feria. I went for a walk, also, last
night. . . ."

"Oh, was that indeed you, Señor? I thought I saw
you, but I was unable to pause. I was seeking for the
daughter of Don Esteban, she who used to be em-
ployed in the infirmary at Ameca, to ask her to come
help my mother. Did you enjoy your walk, Señor?"

He looked at her, and she returned his look with
her usual one of docile incomprehension. "Not
very."

"Ah, no? It is insalubrious to walk much at night.
The air of night is most unhealthy. Dispense me,
Señor, I must mix the tamale dough in this little
moment."

He said, gloomily, "Go with God."

Lupita went, but not with the God that Jacob had
in mind. She mixed her dough and prepared the
fillings and put the water on to boil after having made
a little steambath in the pot, with a fire of twigs and
torn newspapers. She was the servant of the gringos, and if she were not the servant of the gringos
she would be the servant of others who were no

better. All her life she had been someone's servant, someone else's servant, sweeping the dung from their stables and washing their floors and their dishes. Those who gave her orders wore shoes, but she had worn no shoes. Those sat in chairs while she, when she could snatch the time, squatted on the ground. They could read, she could not; they spoke the tongue of the *blanco* as a birthright, she had never fully mastered it. They spoke much of church, scorning the poor Tenochas of the *Barrio Occidental* for paganism, but although many of them had lain with her none would ever marry her in church. And was not the church a thing of the *blanco*, anyway? What were all these others, *mestizos* in blood, but imitation-*blancos?*

And this had gone on for over four hundred years and for four hundred years a little handful among the Tenocha, the true Aztec blood, had preserved their faith that it would go on forever. Now this faith was being vindicated! The old Axteca gods were returning, had already established their base upon the sacred slopes of Ixta—Huitzilopochtli, Quetzalcoatl, Xiutecuhtli, Ometecuhtli, and Omecihuatl, Mictlantecuhtli and Mictlancihuatl, Tezcatlipoca, and the others—she recited their potent names which hissed and writhed like serpents and clapped and roared like thunders! They were returning to reclaim their land and redeem their people, to drive out *blanco* and *güerro* and *mestizo* alike, put down the upstart and inferior tribes whose fathers the fathers of the Tenocha-Aztecas had conquered, and restore all

things as before. . . . Resistance? Of course there
would be resistance! All the better!

For resistance meant prisoners, hecatombs and
hecatombs of them, and prisoners meant sacrifices,
and sacrifices meant infinitely long and blessedly
endless lines of bound forms being dragged up the
steps of the pyramids and cast upon the altar stones in
such a manner as to arch their chests and make easier
the task of the priests who with one stroke of the
obsidian knife would part skin and flesh and with the
other hand reach in and seize and rip out the beating
heart and deposit it in the bloody basin as food for the
gods—ah!—ah!

But not a gleam of this inner exultation disturbed
the meek and stolid passivity of Lupita's face as she
continued her work. She, humble and lame Lupita,
would nevertheless and at a near time become a
priestess . . . a princess . . . a, perhaps,
queen. . . . She was uncertain of the precise title,
but it was not important, not at all important. What
was important was *blood*—blood from the pulsating,
smoking heart, containing the essence of life, the
source of the mystic power of the gods, the benefits
of which would accrue to all the gods' people: yes!
And no more such trifling tidbits as the hearts of kids
or of cats, but the hearts of *men!* Men of inferior
Indian tribes, mestizo men, blanco men. . . . A
very faint gleam showed in her dull black eyes. She
was thinking of how they would tremble and how
they would plead and, finally, of how they would
scream.

"Does the water now cook and steam, Señora?"
she inquired.

"Yes, Lupita."

"Bueno. . . ."

Soon, soon, she would serve the gods a proper
godly food. Once again she recited their sonorous
names. An almost imperceptible droop came to her
lower lip. One god was still missing of the sacred
company, and until he was present the re-Conquest
could not be carried out. But this would not be long.
It was known where he slumbered, and soon he, too,
would be awakened.

Tlaloc! Tlaloc!

Luis rose slowly and delightfully from the depths of
his slumber, drifting at leisure into waking. The
vague lineaments of his recent dreams melted into
golden mists. They had been greatly pleasant, that
was enough. He was not totally awake as yet, but he
knew that he was waking. So be it. All was well. In a
moment . . . more or less . . . he would open his
eyes. . . .

It was a long moment, and he smiled to see that he
didn't recall where he was. Some rustic shack. It
would all come back to him in a moment, the name of
the girl, the memory of her *pro forma* reluctance, and
how without her little sighs and cries ceasing for
more than a moment the nature and message of them
had changed completely. . . . He sat up very suddenly and his mouth fell open. There was no girl and
there had been no girl, not last night, he had been

telescoping time and thinking of a rural amour of a
month or so ago. What then *had* happened last night?

The delights of slumber and false memory ebbed
fast, and, to his astonishment, he sobbed and was
seized by a little tremor of fright. His hand clutched
something in a reflexive spasm, he opened his hand
to see what it was—

—A piece of gold about as long as a cigarette and
about as wide and thick as a small box of wax
matches, but tapering at each end, with one end
pierced and strung upon a cord of maguey fiber—

—The side facing him was smooth and blank; he
turned it over and saw a spotted animal head, very
stylized, with fangs bared: *ocelotl:* one of the puissant symbols of the Great Old Ones, They Who Had
Ruled Before The Tenocha.

And it was They who had given it to him. He
remembered all of this now and his fright vanished
away. Once again he felt fine, excellently fine. *Take
health and take rest.* . . . His left leg, injured in a
fight two years back, and which had begun to ache
yesterday from all that climbing, no longer ached—
in fact, his eyes and fingers now confirmed, the long
dark dull scar itself was quite gone and the brown
skin where it had been glowed with health. Furthermore, one of his canines, always inclined to be a
"bad" tooth, had lately seemed both loose and
twinging: now it was neither.

Health and rest. . . . He had received both, no
doubt of that.

The hut he was in was unremarkable, a pile of

mats and a sheepskin for a bed. Next to that on
another and smaller mat was a small brown earthen
mug of *atole*-gruel and the familiar small basket
containing a napkin with warm tortillas and bean
paste. The gruel was still warm, too. So. . . . He
ate and sipped and reflected. They had said, the
Great Old Ones, that they would see him and talk
with him and answer his questions another time. But
they had not named when that time would be. So
. . . *entonces* . . . he, Luis, was going to decide
that time. Now . . . or as near to now as it would
take him to find them. True, he could not force them.
If it was their pleasure to put him asleep again, he
would be put to sleep again: *nada más*. And maybe
again and again. But eventually they would tire of it
and then the moment of true confrontation was
bound to arise.

He went out of the hut and stopped to urinate and
while he was doing so he looked all around him.
There, *there* was San Juan Bautista Moxtomí, not
more than a quarter mile away as the hawk flies . . .
but Luis, keenly aware that he was not a hawk, knew
that it was a good hour's walk from where he now
stood. Besides, he had no desire to go there now, it
looked its usual sleepy self, with the woodsmoke
escaping through the open eaves and the only sign of
life the figure of a man who was doubtless engaged in
the same simple necessity as he himself. Which
necessity being concluded, Luis buttoned himself up
and started to walk. He had two of the tortillas in his
pocket and he might find something on or under the
fruit and nut trees which were said to be still bearing

(although not well or abundantly) around the ruins of the old hacienda which had been stormed and burned during the Revolution when the Zapatistas came pouring up from Cuautla. Possibly a corner of roof and wall were yet standing, and he just might shelter there if bad weather set in—

One never knew, so close to Popo, when squalls of snow might not descend. One *did* know, though, that beyond the ruins there was no human habitation in any condition on this side of the mountain. And it was thither that he was bound, up through the woods and up through the forests, over the fallen rocks and trees and over the gorges, up into the dominions of the wolf and the eagle and the bear, up into the black and barren volcanic sand which fringed Popocatapetl like a trailing mantle, up the snowy sides by narrow and twisting trails, over the flanks of ice, until— if need be, if he lived to get that far—over the frozen lips of the crater and down, down, down, into the slumbering, but still vulcanous, depths inside. . . .

As far as he had to go, that far he would go, but he would find those he sought after.

If he lived.

Luis took the paths more or less as he found them, as long as they went in the general direction of his goal. Where there were no paths heading upwards he struck out across the unmarked land that was open. From time to time he saw the last settlement dwindle in size and finally vanish away altogether. Once, looking down, he saw the shadows of the clouds pacing across a great valley, and, finally, he was able to look down upon clouds themselves; and at last he looked down upon the hawks and the eagles as they wheeled and circled and sought their meat from God.

The trees became fewer, the bare bones of the earth thrust up at him, the air grew thin and chill. He walked very close to the side of the rock-face now, and avoided further looks down into the deep gorge. And when he heard the growl and snarl of the beast and felt his male flesh shrink in upon itself and his heart swell in cold fear even before he, edging around a turn in the trail, saw the great golden eyes and the golden pelt spotted with black markings and the lips drawn back from the teeth—

He felt in his bones, cold fingers upon cold skin, and drew out the amulet, the sign of the Great Old Ones, and held it out as far as the cord would reach. The jaguar gazed at it, gold reflected into gold. The jaguar bowed his head down upon its paws. The jaguar retreated. When Luis made the next turn it was gone. It could have neither gone up nor down and even if it had gone back it would still be visible. But, of course, it was no ordinary jaguar, as he had known from the first, for this was not the natural habitat of such. It was the magic jaguar of the Olmec, it was a guardian beast. . . .

Coming out upon a broad and bare plateau, he could not resist removing the loop from around his neck and fondling and admiring the amulet. It was gold, it was certainly gold, but it was not as heavy as gold should be, and he wondered if it was partly hollow—and why.

The first shout and shot startled him. He cried out, the object slipped, his lunge for it missed, he saw it fall and jumped for it. The second shot spun him around and spun the world around and he saw the darkness close in and the shouts became a roar. He crawled, with the weight of the whirling world upon him, seized and grasped the *ocelotl*, and surrendered to the clamoring dark.

VII

He smelled the sour, stale stink of them . . . old sweat, old clothes, old pulque, and something else . . . worse than any of the others . . . his mind tried to identify this. Why, he could not say, particularly since part of his mind was aware that with some effort he could identify at least which puzzled him—and then recognition came: it was the evil, fishy reek of old blood, like a butcher who hasn't changed his apron for days. So.

That done, now to the voices. He did not know them well at all, but he did know them . . . that is, he knew that he had heard them. The memory was neither clear nor pleasant. He kept his eyes closed.

"A nice piece of venison," said one, poking a thick finger into Luis's ribs. An ordinary voice, this one.

"Not dead, I hope?" This one was hoarse and phlegmy, one of the familiar ones—and, whereas the first comment had been made in Spanish, this second

was in Nahua. And now the first one spoke again,
and in Nahua, too.

"I don't think so. . . ." A hand was laid roughly
on Luis's heart. "No . . . this is still good. . . ."
The all but imperceptible pause was succeeded by a
sigh of genuine longing, such as one might hear from
a mother awaiting her long-delayed child or a woman
yearning for the arms of a distant lover. It was not at
all the sort of sound which one might expect to hear
from the man, whoever he was or whatever he was,
with the ordinary voice.

And now a third voice spoke, a thin and whining
sort, this. "What is one? One is nothing, nothing at
all. There must be hundreds, thousands!"

The hoarse one said, "Everything starts with one
thing—*Vamanos!*" he concluded, abruptly. They
tied Luis hand and foot and one of them tossed him
over a shoulder as though he were a sack of cobs, and
jogged off, the others (as Luis could hear) trotting
alongside. It was almost insufferably uncomfort-
able, but he would hardly expect that anyone would
shoot at him with the intention of subsequently buy-
ing him a ride on a *primera clase* bus. Furthermore,
he had something else to occupy his mind besides his
discomfort.

It was the last word that had done it, supplied the
key. What the man's name was, he didn't remember,
perhaps had never known. But he knew now who he
was—the barrel-shaped, frog-faced fellow who pre-
sided every Saturday and Sunday in the marketplace
over a caldron of hog-*tripas* frying in dirty, viscid oil

. . . and spent the rest of the week holding up the wall in one of the filthy pulquerias of the *Barrio Occidental*. Hardly anyone except his fellow slummy neighbors bought the evil-smelling chitterlings, and it was his habit, as he slapped each leathery-looking portion, oozing oil, into a piece of paper, to shout, as though encouraging the next customer, "*¡Vamanos!*" — "Let's go!" Ruiz. His name was Ruiz.

His going and the going of his comrades of course made a complete nothing of all of Luis's goings since he had started that morning. But his regret in this was swallowed up in the thudding of his blood in his ears—however far they were intending to take him, he might not be alive if he continued to be half upside-down as he was now. A genuine groan escaped his lips and he did not attempt to prevent it. The jogging stopped, abruptly, and he was dumped onto the ground.

"Come to, have you?" the gut-fryer asked. Luis nodded. "*Bueno.* Then you can walk by yourself. . . ." He knelt with a grunt and loosened the cord at Luis's ankles. "Walk, that's what I said. Try running, and you'll get some lead sauce for your *tortas.*" He gestured towards the old rifle held in the arm of one of his friends, a rat-faced fellow.

"Let's kill him right now," said Rat Face—in Nahua.

Luis just sighed and rubbed his head with his fists.

"Doesn't understand," Rat Face said.

The third, he of the ordinary voice and by his looks

an ordinary *Barrio Occidental* lounger-around,
probably supported by a washer-woman wife, said,
"How would he understand the Tenocha-talk? Look
at him—wears stockings—probably pretends he's a
blanco puro—father is a landowner—grandmother
was a dirty Moxtomí—"

The three of them spat. *"Vamanos,"* said Hog
Guts, giving Luis a kick in the fundament to emphasize his point. They started off once more, perhaps
not so swiftly as before, for if Luis had tried to run his
hobbles would have sent him flying. They were, it
seemed, heading away from Popo . . . but not precisely downhill, either . . . towards Ixta . . . or at
least in that general direction. Who were they? What
did they want with him? Surely, despite it having
been known to at least one of them that his father did
own a *granja*, surely then it must also be known that
it was a small one, only. If it was known, too, as
much about his family that his grandmother was a
Moxtomí, then wouldn't they also realize how very
little favored he was by his father on this very account? That, even if his father could afford to pay a
ransom, he was most unlikely to do so?

But he didn't ask. It was best to say nothing, for
who knew what ideas it might put into their heads!
And with that an idea came into his own head:
perhaps these bravos were in some way connected
with the alleged sulfur-stealers of the crater of
Popo. . . . Frightened away, perhaps, by the presence of the Great Old Ones . . . it could be that they
were for some reason afraid of his, Luis's—well,

what? Betraying their presence to the authorities?
The theory did not hang together well, but it was at
the moment the only other one he could think of.

He was glad, though, that he hadn't revealed that
he knew anything of the Nahua language—Tenocha,
as they called it—Meshika, or Azteca, as others
called it. The threat or proposal to kill him then was
obviously only a ruse to find out if they could speak
together in that tongue without his knowing what
was being said. Keep your ears open, he told himself.

He couldn't think of anything else he could do for
the moment, anyway.

"We should wear the skin for a week," Rat Face was
saying, as they passed through a meadow wet with
distilled mist. "Thus it was done, and was a thing of
great honor, too. That is," he corrected himself,
"*one* of us should wear it for a week."

The man whom Luis had come to think of as
"Ordinario," in a very sharp voice, demanded,
"*Which* one of us?"

Rat Face scowled, and seemed to remember that
he had the rifle. But Hog Guts, in his rough,
mucousy voice, said, "Can't be done now. Whoever
did it would stink like a dead dog. . . . He'd have to
hide out and there aren't enough of us. Wait. There is
going to be plenty of time . . . and plenty of skins,
too."

Ordinario grunted his agreement. Rat Face once
again uttered his blissful sigh, and the look of one

who sees a beatific vision settled on his face and
almost made it good to look upon.

Luis was not sure what they were talking about.
He knew that there were many pagan cult ceremonies
involving in one way or another the wearing of
animal skins—coyotes or deer, for example. But he
had never heard of anyone wearing such a skin for a
week, or why, even so, he would "stink like a dead
dog" . . . unless the skin hadn't been well-tanned
first. Nor could he imagine what kind of dance or
ritual they could have in mind in speaking of "plenty
of skins" at some future date. It was a mystery.
Perhaps he just didn't know Nahuatl well enough;
there might be idioms and usages . . . for example,
the curious phrase used by the man who had felt his
heart to see if it was beating: *This is still a good
one* . . .

But let it mean what it might; it all added up to
something which he had felt for a long time, that no
good thing ever came out of Aztec land. The Tenochas had been barbarians in the beginning and they
were still barbarians now. And bigots as well.
"Dirty Moxtomí" indeed! As though the Moxtomí
had not been partners in the grandeur and greatness
of the Olmecs and Toltecs at a time when the
Tenocha-Aztecas had been named snake-eaters in
the remote and barbarous deserts of the north! *Pues*
. . . they would see soon enough . . . the Great Old
Ones had returned and soon would, he had no doubt,
impose their victorious rule over all the land. And
then—once those of *Hispanidad* had been ex-
pelled—then the Moxtomí would gain their right-

ful place as inevitably as water seeks its own level;
Tenocha-Azteca would remain as they were and de-
served to be.

This sequence of thoughts comforted him all the
way along to the *baranca*. This gorge twisted like a
snake; Luis was totally unfamiliar with it, as he was
with the small bowl-shaped valley to which it eventually led. And he was totally unprepared for what he
saw.

He was, had been, of course, as familiar with
pictures of Aztec temples and pyramids as a Greek is
with the Acropolis or an Egyptian with the Pyramids.
But this was no picture; this was no ruin. These
walls, this temple, this pyramid, were—true—
exceedingly old . . . they seemed to be older than
the old church in Los Remedios . . . but they were
in at least as good a state of preservation. He stood
stock-still and stunned, and scarcely noticed when
the cord around his ankles was removed and retied
with almost no slack at all. The structures he saw
now, here contained an unmistakable message: that
in this place from a time before the Conquest of
Mexico by the Spaniards, throughout the centuries of
blanco rule, the centuries of Christian supremacy,
this temple to the Aztec cult had been secretly and
successfully maintained and preserved.

And when he reflected on that cult and all that it
implied, his flesh turned cold and began to tremble.

His captors removed their clothes and dressed
again in loincloths and mantles and headdresses of
antique design. They drew water in a vessel of Aztec
pattern and sprinkled it about the courtyard, chanting

things in a form of High Nahuatl which he did not
fully understand. Next they poured libations of pulque, then they built and kindled a fire, then they
danced about it, singing, and in the course of this
they drew embers from the fire into an incense burner
and cast beads of odorous copal-gum upon it. Back
and forth, around and around, in a pattern which
grew increasingly more intricate, the three men
danced, their voices growing louder and louder.

"Tezcatlipoca-Titlacaoan: We are his slaves!
Shining Mirror, Smoking Mirror, Moon of the
Night Sky,
Ruler of Darkness, Dreams, Phantoms, and the
Coyotes of the Gloom . . .
Quetzalcoatl: Plumed Serpent, Sweeper of the
Way!
Conqueror of The Sun, Supporter of the
Sky . . .
Huitzilopochtli, Bright Hummingbird,
Dragon's-head!
Drinker of the Rivers of Blood, Slayer of
Enemies,
Lover of Many Hearts, Great Face, Burning
Eyes . . .
Tonantzin-Cihuacoatl Our Mother, Woman of
the Serpent!
Scatterer of Seeds, Feeder of Wild Beasts . . .
Tlaculteotl, Provoker of Passion and Lust!
All Ye Potent Ones, Guides of Our Fathers,
Delighters in the Sacrifices,

Attend to us,
Hearken,
Come!''

The three dancing men lifted up their heads, threw back their heads, howling like beasts, gashing their tongues and their earlobes till the blood ran. They threw themselves upon their knees and struck their heads upon the smooth paving stones. From within the temple a horn of some sort sounded and blared. Luis, with staring eyes and trembling breath, saw a movement at the temple door. And then the great and terrible gods of the Aztecs appeared and then he screamed and screamed and screamed.

"All is prepared," the inhuman voice of Huit-zilopochtli declared. "All, or almost all. The mirror is polished, the way has been swept, the weapons are prepared, the faithful await the summons, the cords are knotted and the knife is sharpened and the fire is prepared. The only thing which lacks is the Great Heart—"

The other gods brayed and groaned and clamored and stamped their feet and brandished their war clubs and their incense burners. Their eyes burned in the grotesque masks of their faces, their plumes waved, their tusks clashed.

"—the Great Heart of Tlaloc-Tlamacazqui: Only this is lacking!"

The three men rose to their feet and resumed their dance and their chant.

"Tlaloc-Tlamacazqui, Giver of Rain!
Moistener of the Earth, Donor of Hail and
    Lightning,
Sender of Storms and Perils on River and Sea,
Dweller in Paradise,
Attend to us,
Hearken,
Come!"

But Huitzilopochtli and his fellows seemingly did not delight in this invocation; they advanced with menacing cries and gestures. The dancing and chanting stopped, the three worshippers crouched contritely, placing their palms upon the ground and raising them to their lips and kissing them. The ground round about them was stained with their blood.

"Have you not heard? Have you not understood? It is vain to invoke Our Brother Tlaloc! He is not here and he will not be here until that which we call his Great Heart is found and secured. It is in this region, Slaves of Tezcatlipoca! It is in this area, Servants of Quetzalcoatl! It is not far from here, Warriors of Huitzilopochtli! Sons of Holy Mother Tonantzin and Sacred Sister Tlaculteotl; we tell you that the mirror reveals that it is at no great distance, and we tell you that it must be found!"

The three men sat with their arms around their knees, their eyes cast down. And when Dragon-Headed Huitzilopochtli had finished and his distorted voice was silent, the heavy one said, "O

Drinker of the Rivers of Blood, when it is found, this Puissant Object, then will all proceed as planned?''

"All! All!"

The thin one asked, ''Slayer of Enemies, when it is found, then shall the Tenocha rule over all of Anahuac, all of the Valley of Mexico, as before?''

"All! All!"

He sighed his same blissful, yearning sigh. And Ordinario, in turn: ''Dragon-Head, Great Hummingbird, when it is found, then will the gods be pleased to accept all of our sacrifices and grant us all their benefits as before?''

And for the third and final time, the great beaked muzzle of the Huitzilopochtli parted and the utterly alien voice declared, ''All! All!''

"Why, then, do you tarry?'' it brayed.

They leaped to their feet. ''The Great Heart of Tlaloc, we will find it! And in the meanwhile, O our father's gods, be pleased to accept the finest fruit of the first of our offerings!'' Two of them turned and seized hold of Luis and tore his clothes from him; while he screamed and struggled, the third mounted the pyramid. Luis was borne, kicking and twisting, up the stone steps and thrown and held upon the altar, his pleas and shrieks never ceasing. A stone with a convex surface was under him, so that his chest was thrust up. The thin Tenocha, his face transformed, leaned over and lightly stroked the sweating skin as though to mark the place, then lifted the knife with its blade of curved black obsidian.

"Stay! Hold!"

The Huitzilopochtli itself mounted the steps. Something gleamed in its paw. It seemed simultaneously vexed and puzzled. "We had anticipated the joy and pleasure of tasting heart and of being strengthened by the fluid of life," it said. "But—see—" It was the golden *ocelotl*, just now fallen from Luis's suddenly spastic fingers. "This is a sigil of the so-called Great Old Ones and it is in some way connected and in communion with them. And even though we have often defeated them and driven them away from this and other worlds, and even though it is true that they are indescribably far from this world at present. . . ." He brooded, emitting small squawking sounds from time to time; then the great grotesque head bobbed abruptly, nodded.

"Release him; do not choose him again. Where he obtained a sigil, how many fives of centuries old it may be, I do not know. But inasmuch as our total plans embrace the ultimate and absolute defeat of those Great Old Ones, it is far from our desire that they be made aware of our presence for now. So. Go!" It flung out its hand and stalked stiffly away.

The three men gazed at each other, blinking. They seemed to have awakened from a dream. Then the one with the knife severed Luis's bonds. Another helped him to his feet, and the third restrung the cord with its gleaming symbol about his neck. "The gods have exempted you from sacrifice," they said to him, softly, awed, without resentment. "How you have been honored!" And after a ceremonial leave-taking, they helped him rearrange his tattered clothing and conducted him respectfully back out of the hidden valley, down the gorge, and far, far down the escarpments of Ixtaccihuatl, until at last their feet touched a much-trodden trail.

"Con permiso," he said, irony upheld by belatedly returned courage.

They looked at him with sober eyes, sarcasm having totally passed them by. *"Pase Vd.,"* they said. And they watched him go, faces only faintly regretful, and totally drained of anger.

There were many things in the mind of Luis as he picked his way down the path. Not smallest of the wonders was the difference between these men as he had known them in their outer appearances, boors and buffoons, dwellers in a despised quarter; and as he saw them now in their innerness, heritors of an antique trust and an ancient, unbounded faith.

But the improvement was one which he felt that he and his fellow countrymen could well afford to do without.

VIII

Tata Santiago Tuc, his nephew Domingo Deuh, and others of the council of the pueblo of San Juan Bautista Moxtomí, sat at the feet of the Great Old Ones. The vast and benign countenances of the latter gazed upon the calm and trusting faces of the Indians.

"It was not by our own wish," explained the Elder Old One, first among equals in their own councils, "that we should leave you. True, that we were pleased to return to our home in the most distant stars, my sons. But we traveled, even then, between here and there with little more difficulty than any of you might travel between Chalco and Cuautla. Often we went, often we returned. We knew the Olmec, we knew the Toltec and the Mixtec and the Maya, as well as the Moxtomí and others. We loved them as our children, they loved us as their fathers; we taught them, they were apt, and learned. And so the maize grew and was harvested, and so the ages passed."

"When the Tenocha, whom some call the Azteca, came down from the north, what were they?"

Tuc answered, his seamed face split by a bitter and contemptuous smile. "A handful of savages, lizard-eaters, knowing nothing of agriculture or of any other of the arts of civilized men. War was all that they knew—only war!"

But as the Aztecs were descending from the north, fighting and butchering as they went; at about this same time the Huitzili were descending on the land from their own home-world among the distant, distant Evil Stars. Few were their own numbers and, at first, small their own resources. But with the cleverness of the wicked they had recognized that the Aztec were a people designed, as it were, by nature to be their tools and the means of their own advancement.

Far, far different was their appearance from the appearance of men, unlike the appearance of the Great Old Ones whose form was like that of giant, exalted men. But the Huitzili were grotesque, horrid, ungainly, distorted . . . Made and suited to impress the rude minds and coarse fantasies of the Aztecs, who at once elevated the Huitzili to the status of gods—

And then, under their guidance and with their aid, proceeded to conquer as they came, until all the lovely land of Anahuac was theirs, and then the adjacent lands, even unto the sea.

The price was, of course, great, for the Huitzili loved the hearts and blood of man-flesh, and literally rivers of it flowed upon their altars. War, which had first been made to gain land and then to get tribute, continued after both land and tribute was guaranteed . . . *had* to continue, for only from the multitudes of prisoners could come the requisite number of human sacrifices. And thus, as the power of the Aztecs increased, so did the power of their gods, their allies, the Huitzili.

"War was not our own talent," said the Elder Old One. "And after each encounter we continued in our previous ways, expecting each time that life would be as it was before, that now at last the Huitzili would menace no more. But, by the time we had realized that the Huitzili would always menace because it was a structural part of their nature to do so, events in and around our own world prevented us from full-scale resistance here on this world. But we did what we could. . . .

"We lured them away. . . .

"To assure our children here of at least some continued benefits, we hid that goodly thing which has been called the Great Heart of Tlaloc, we set an appointed guardian and watcher over it—"

Domingo Deuh said in a low and breathy voice, "*El* Heremito Sagrado. . . ."

"The Guardian was in the shape of an ordinary man, the humble custodian of a humble Indian shrine located over and above the cavern where the Tlaloc-which-contained-the-Great-Heart-of-Tlaloc was located. The presumption was that none would look for it in so obvious a place, and this presumption had proved correct. The Great Old

Ones fled, luring the Huitzili with them. For long
ages chase, pursuit, encounter, fight, between the
two forces continued. Meanwhile, here in Anahuac,
the unforeseen had happened. The Azteca-Tenocha
did not—deprived of Huitzili guidance—crumble
and fall apart. Their momentum carried them on to
further conquests; unable to offer human blood and
human hearts to their actual and present gods, they
continued nonetheless to offer them up before the
idols and the images. And the butchery and blood-
bath continued. . . .

"Then came the Spaniards, who, with the aid of
many of the subject tribes and nations of Mexico,
destroyed the Aztec power forever. True, they intro-
duced a new bondage, but it had not the same stench
of rotten blood about it as the old one had. And the
Guardian appraised this new situation and he met it
well; he himself embraced the new faith and under
his influence most of the other local Indians embraced it as well. As a result, he was able to remain
where he had been; eventually he 'died.' . . . But,
as he had foreseen, even in his 'death' he was able to
continue on guard. The legends which grew up
around him, of course, helped in his task. If he rose
from his bier in the night to inspect the cavern where
the object was concealed, the whisper went around
that he had miraculously been transported to Rome to
serve the Pope at mass. . . .

"But one group of local Indians had never trusted
him, never accepted him, loved nor venerated him;
and these were the descendants of the local Aztec

priests of the bloody sacrifices, who—decayed and downtrodden, sullen and suspicious—still lived in the *Barrio Occidental.*''

Old Santiago Tuc nodded his head. *"Sí, Viejo Poderoso* . . . it is true. That is why they would try to capture his catafalque during the procession each year. They believed that this would help them to find where the Great Heart was hidden. And then they would have the key to open and to close the rain and then they would make all of Anahuac do their bidding.'' He sighed and groaned. ''It is known and revealed how we Moxtomí have suffered since the Spaniards came. Generation after generation we have lost some of our communal lands— confiscation, sequestration, rectification of boundaries, taxation—what names haven't they used! They have eaten our lands like a child eats *gomitas.* The King, the Viceroy, the First Republic, the First Emperor, then Santa Anna, then our good Juarez, the Second Emperor, again Juarez, Diaz, revolution, revolution. . . . Now and then we regained a little *milpita* here or there, but mostly it has been loss. . . .

''Still, *Viejo Poderoso,* though we hold only a handful of our *ejido* lands, it is better than being flung upon the altars of the vile Tenochas, to have our hearts cut out and our skins flayed off ! *Ai!* I do not know what powers the Huitzili still may have, or how such power may compare to the military and air force and the armada of Mexico. I have heard it said, though, that it matters but little to the pitcher whether it is dropped upon the stone or if the stone is dropped upon the pitcher. We do not want war, we do not want sacrifices, we do not want drought. We want only our old *ejido* lands—and if we cannot have them back, then let us at least have peace. We look to you, Great Old One, to save us from this present threat.''

A faint and infinitely patient smile passed across the massy features of the Elder Old One. "We hope you do not look in vain. . . .There is, we must tell you, more at stake here besides Anahuac. In the Great Heart of Tlaloc—and need I tell you that it is not indeed a real heart—that it is, how shall I compare it, an engine, a device of infinite power and infinite potency, such as our own much reduced capacities are no longer capable of replacing . . . dwindled as we are from centuries of combat—in the Great Heart of Tlaloc lies more than the ability to insure rain. In it lies the means of turning life to death, matter to not-matter. Should the Huitzili succeed in capturing and mastering it, not Anahuac alone, but the entire universe may well be helpless before them. The struggle between us has been costly to them as well as to us. The few of them who are here once again, once again masquerading as gods, are all of them that are anywhere.

"This is their last chance!"

Some of the men spoke in favor of proceeding at once, then, to seize and remove the Great Heart from where it had so long lain concealed. But others counseled caution. "It is not the Huitzili alone who are sniffing like dogs," Domingo Deuh pointed out.

"They know that the Great Heart exists, but they do not—*yet*—know that it is hidden inside the Tlaloc under the Monte Sagrado.

"But the government has sent troops—the government is going to remove the Tlaloc and take it to the new Big House of Old Things in 'Mexico'—but the government and the military does not know—*yet*—that anything is inside of it. Many of the people in the district are very uneasy, and say that if Tlaloc is moved then there will be no more rain within the whole land of Anahuac, that is, the Valley of Mexico. And, they, too, stirred up as they are without fully realizing the whole of the matter, may prove a danger."

The huge head of the Elder Old One slowly went down and as slowly came up again. "Then we must move," he said, "not only as swiftly as possible, but as secretly as possible." His great golden eyes sought those of his fellows, and, as slowly and deliberately, they nodded as well.

A wind, chill and pure from the heights of the snowy mountains, came through the village and shook the cedar trees until the air was filled with their rustling.

"Let it be done. Let it be done. *Let it be done*."

Jacob Clay nibbled at his pipe and stared at his typewriter. Truthfully, he had no inspiration for writing anything at all at the moment and the long hours he had put in on the manuscript just completed had depleted his nervous energy to the point where he felt

in need of rest. How nice it would be to throw a few
things into a *bolsa* and take off for a few days in, say,
Cuautla, or Cuernavaca! But this dream died aborn-
ing. They were too broke. And even though nothing
he could begin writing now could possibly bring in
any money soon enough to take the vacation while he
was feeling the need of it, still, conscience would not
allow him just to say "The Hell with it!" and have
Sarah pack a picnic lunch which they could eat in the
arcadian beauty alongside one of the little rivers. In
short, the time would just go for nothing—unless,
most unlikely, the Paraclete would be pleased to
descend after all, with an Idea clasped in its bill like
an olive branch.

"*Bienvenida*, Luis," he called out, thankful for
an excuse, as he saw the young man hesitating in the
patio. "Come on in . . . sit down. . . ."

"Jacobo, you are not too busy?"

"No, no. All the time in the world."

"But I think maybe you are too busy. I was rudely
bothering you the last occasions."

Jacob winced. "No . . . I'm afraid that I was the
rude one then. But then I was busy and now I'm
really not. Take a chair, please."

They looked at each other, smiled a trifle con-
strainedly, said nothing. Finally, Jacob, to break the
ice, said, almost without considering, "Luis, have
you ever heard of any kind of club or cult or something which meets in the woods up there and then
some of them dress up in coyote skins and the others
dress up like the old Aztec gods? Have you ever

heard of—'' He broke off. Then he said, "Oh. You have. Well. I see. I'm sorry I mentioned it. I see by your face that I shouldn't have. *Dispenseme*."

Luis touched his tongue to his lips, swallowed. "No. No, Jacobo, it isn't that you—Jacobo, Jacobo! They do not dress up like. No, ah, no— They *are* the old Aztec gods! Very terrible! *Ai de mi!*"

"You've seen them, too, then? But you're not one of the, mmm, worshippers, then? No. Good. . . . 'Terrible'? Christ, yes! Gave me the creeping meemies. But, now, Luis, when you say that those characters really *are* the old Aztec gods, well, come on now! You know better than that, for crying out loud. You've been to school."

Luis stretched out his hands, automatically beginning to gesticulate, and Jacob's eyes saw the marks on his wrists. Luis saw that he saw, and exposed his ankles as well. Jacob grunted. "Ah, these are nothing, the marks are already fading and will be soon gone, thanks to the power of the *sigilo* of the Great Old Ones, *Los Viejos Poderosos*. They gave me this, you see?" He opened his shirt, and there against the tan skin of his chest was the golden object with the ocelot's head.

Jacob peered at it. "This sure looks old," he said. "I'm no judge of such things, really, but it does look very old . . . Toltec, maybe . . . or maybe even Olmec. . . . Where did you get it, Luis?"

And Luis, talking more rapidly than quite coherently, told him of the Great Old Ones who were now returned and had their place on, or in, or perhaps

only very, very near Popo—and of the also latterly
returned Aztec gods, and what they had tried to do
and almost did do to him a while back that day.
"They fear the power of the Great Old Ones, Jacobo!
They fear them, but they do not yet know that the
Great Old Ones are already here."

Jacob got up. "Well. . . . Something is sure as
hell going on that's not strictly kosher. Tell you
what. Let's go talk about this to Macauley. What do
you say?"

Luis's face lit up. "Bueno! Excellent. Don Roberto is a very good person to consult. He knows
much of all the *costumbres* of the countryside, and of
our history as well. Good, good!" He almost danced
in his excitement.

Jacob knocked on the window of the living room
to attract Sarah's attention. She looked up, her face
tear-stained and abstract. She was engaged in painting a picture from memory of poor sweet-tootsie-
little Evans.

"Luis and I are going over to Mac to see him about
that business of last night."

"Oh. . . . All right, dear. . . ."

"We may not be back till quite late, I don't know.
Be sure to lock and bolt all the doors, particularly the
back one into our patio. I'll get in from the front
patio. Okay?"

"Oh. . . . All right, dear. . . ."

She had forgotten all about him by the time the
door to the front patio had closed. How fortunate that
she had thought to bring these paints and papers with

her. And that she'd gotten the idea to do this picture while his little memory was still fresh in her mind—not that it could ever possibly fade!—but still. . . . She brushed her hair back, absentmindedly smearing her face with paint. Then she smiled fondly as she looked at the outlined figure on the paper. Perhaps a black background, to show off his white markings? No . . . that would never do . . . it would fail to show off his *black* markings. Blue, perhaps . . . or red. . . . Blue would go best with his poor little golden eyes.

Sarah bent over her portrait.

Sometime later she looked up, aware of being faintly disturbed by something. What was it? Hunger, that was it. The tamales had been very good. Perhaps some of them were still left. But would Jacob want some? No, Jacob had gone to Mac's place and he said he'd be there quite late, which meant that he would eat as well as talk. Sarah got up slowly, considering. Heat up some tamales . . . and what else? Not much, of course. . . . Maybe a few tostados. Nothing heavy. Cheese, perhaps. And a little salad on the side. A cup of tea. And a *pastelito*, if there were any. Perhaps a piece of fruit.

People had to *eat;* they had to keep their strength up, even if their hearts were just *breaking*. Look at all those rich, yummy recipes Martha Washington was always working on. She probably had cried *buckets* while George and those tootsie soldiers were freezing their toes at Valley Forge, but *that* didn't

prevent her from trying out a new way to make
pound-cake, did it? Although, when you come right
down to it—Sarah moved into the kitchen—what it
was that George *saw* in her, well, really. *"She's*
nothing to look at, wouldn't you agree?"* Sarah
asked aloud of no one in particular.

Certainly of no one in the kitchen, for there *was* no
one in the kitchen. Oh, well. She would toss up her
little meal by herself. She looked around for pots and
pans and utensils and dishes. There were none.
"Hasn't Lupita finished washing them *yet?"* she
exclaimed. And went, frowning, out into the patio.
The dishes and pots and other utensils were there all
right, grease and all, in the concrete sink by the water
barrel. Only Lupita was not there.

"La Lupita?" repeated the landlady, looking a bit
displeased. Yes, Lupita had been seen. First, *el
joven* Luis had gone into the *oficina* of Don Jacobo.
Then, la Lupita, the without-shame, had been per-
ceived to listen at the door. Then she had left the
patio—"going very, very rapidly"—and the house,
and disappeared into the streets. *Donde?* "Ah,
where indeed? Who knows? The Señora would be
well-advised to examine well among her own pos-
sessions, to see if la Lupita did not have 'little
hands.' "

The usually most pleasant landlady struggled with
her feelings, finally admitted, "She is neither amiable nor sympathetic, that girl."

Sarah gave a small moan. "Do thou was knowing
also possibly to have another girl for employer more
responsible?" she inquired.

Señora Mariana shrugged, threw out her hands. "Ah, poor lady! But these girls today prefer to go to 'Mexico' to seek employment, because there they can obtain more pesos." She quirked her mouth and made a circle with thumb and forefinger to indicate the roundness of the peso. But more than this she was unable to do.

Sarah returned, slowly, and lugubriously. She reheated the tamales and ate them, somberly. Then she went out and looked at the pile of dirty, greasy dishes and pots again. She tested the water with her little finger. It was very, very cold.

Mac, advised in English that a matter of the gravest importance was to be discussed, had sent his lady friend and her ancient aunt out to buy pulque, and grilled *carnitas*. "Be sure to hurry there and back," he had told them.

The lady scowled. "Securely, we will sprout wings like the birds and fly," she said. "With the gringos it is always, *pronto, pronto, pronto!*"

As they left, twitching their rebozos indignantly, he smiled at his guests. "That should insure us at least an hour. . . . So. What's up, Doc?"

Jacob sighed. "Well. . . . It doesn't sound as crazy to me as it would have yesterday. But . . . well . . . Luis claims that those oddballs in the boondocks, the Aztec-god ones, I mean . . . he claims that they captured him early today and tried to turn him into a human sacrifice. The cardiectomy clinic—just like you said."

Macauley pursed his lips and let out his breath in a

near-whistle, so that his golden mustache floated up. "Well, well," he murmured. Then he turned to face Luis. *"Digame,"* he ordered.

Luis, after hesitations and stumbling starts, began by recapitulating the various rumors sweeping the town on the eve of the fiera of the Holy Hermit: that lights had been seen on both Popo and Ixta, that the government was going to take away the Tlaloc from under the Monte Sagrado, that smoke had been seen rising from Popo, that soldiers were in town on an unholy mission, that there would be trouble with the procession, that the abominable *Naguales,* or were-coyotes, had been seen once more, and so on.

He described his visit to the Moxtomí pueblo, San Juan Bautista, in hopes of discussing these rumors—how he found them in an uproar, how they put him off. He described the fight, the genuine and not symbolic attempt to seize the catafalque as it passed through the *Barrio Occidental,* and then: "And then, *hombre!* My word of honor! The catafalque fell and the Hermit tumbled out and then he walked away—*he walked away!"*

And so all the other details came out, how the Hermit was really the long-time Guardian of the Entrusted Object and how the Entrusted Object was the Heart of Tlaloc, only it was not really a heart; how the true or false "Aztec gods," the Huitzili, were, like the pseudo-gods of the old Olmec and Toltec days, really denizens of other and distant worlds . . . detail by incredible detail, the story emerged.

Macauley chewed the ends of his long mustaches. "Wow, boy," he said. "Well, Jake, I think we've got two choices, count 'em, two. The first is that Luis's story is the real McCoy, the clean quill, weird and way-out as it is. And the other is that *some*body out there"—his hand gestured toward the wild uplands crowned by the snowy sierra of Ixtaccihuatl and the shining cone of Popocatapetl—"has (a) been reading one hell of a lot of science fiction, and (b) been spending one hell of a lot of time and money and effort. . . .

"On the whole," he said, thoughtfully reaching for his gigantic mustache-cup of coffee, "on the whole, I tend to think that the first one proposes far fewer problems."

Jacob asked, "What's to do about it, then?"

Macauley smiled. "Find out about it! I wouldn't go near that pseudo-Aztec crowd with a ten-foot ack-ack gun. But Luis seems impressed with the good will of the pseudo-Olmec/Toltec boys. I vote that we take a nice hike up in the general direction of Uncle Popo and see what we can see."

The vote went with *aye*.

Jacob, afterwards, was not sure that it should not have been *ai!*

Huitzilopochtli blared and brayed his rage and his delight. "You have done well, you have done well, woman!" His Dragon-Head and blunt-beaked muzzle darted up and down. "We have returned to reward you all and we will reward you all, but we have

also returned in that we are necessitous of obtaining
once and for all the Great Heart of Tlaloc. And now
that we know that the Great Old Ones, our enemies,
have returned as well, it is certain that we know that
they, too, seek this Puissant Object. They know
where it is—they must know! For it is they who
malignantly concealed it in the first place!''

And his fellows stamped and howled and it was
agreed by all of them that they would go up to Popo
and espy out all there was to espy, and then decide on
what was to be done.

And thus it was Jacob and Macauley and Luis
were observed as they climbed. And were followed,
as the sun sank and the shadows grew.

_IX_

The immense golden-bronze bell voice of the Elder Old One was raised but a single note, yet it seemed that all the sounds of the forest and the night fell silent and hearkened to it. "We have not been here long," he said, "nevertheless, we have been here long enough. Both the lights and the smokes of our vessel have been seen on Popo. There has been talk, suspicion must follow, eventually attempts to investigate will be made. I believe it would not be well for our star-ship to be seen where it is concealed within the upper crater of the mountain which once smoked itself."

The lids of his benign eyes lifted but a trifle more, the golden and glowing pupils flashed a message to his fellows and to the Moxtomí. "The synchronism of events is disturbing. It cannot be helped that both the Huitzili-things and the forces of the present government of this land are both now intent upon the same mission as we are, though for far different

reasons. The alien and evil enemy may begin at any
time to proceed against the hidden Object. We know
what time the military intends to begin: tomorrow.

"I say that we have, accordingly, only this single
night in which to accomplish our intention. If any
have reason to gainsay me: speak. I wait. I listen."

The night was silent, the fire glowed, reflecting
glowing sparks in both the golden eyes and the
brown ones. Old Santiago Tuc said at length, "I
know of nothing that we Moxtomí, your servants,
can say against your words. Go, *Viejos
Poderosos*—go, Lords, and we will follow."

The lips of the Great Old Ones moved in mild
smiles and their eyes exchanged consent. Their
senior said, gently, "It will be in this way, younger
brothers: let the Moxtomí go before, as befits their
position of prime dwellers in this land. And *we* will
follow."

Old Tuc rose from his haunches and fell upon his
knees. "It is too much honor," he murmured. Then
he got to his feet and gave crisp orders, pointing with
his finger and naming names. In a very few moments
only, the pueblo of San Juan Bautista Moxtomí was
left in the charge of its women and children and
patron saint. And the silent night was penetrated by
the slight but sustained sounds of marching feet.
Domingo Deuh went before, with a torch in one hand
and a spear, formed of a knife lashed to a pole, in the
other. Behind him came *Tata* Tuc, holding a censer
of burning coals of the old pre-Spanish fashion in one
piece, and a pouch of beads of copal-gum, from
which he, from time to time, took a pinch and cast it

on the embers. Behind him came a man with the pueblo's single shotgun, then the other men, armed with clubs, knives, and improvised but, nonetheless, deadly spears.

And behind them, carrying nothing which the Moxtomí knew to be weapons, but serene and utterly self-confident, huge bodies and massive limbs, towering so high that they now and then were obliged to lift their hands and push away thick and overhanging limbs as though they were mere twigs, came the Great Old Ones.

They wore only what seemed to be the lightest of garments and the Indians were swathed from chin to calf in thick, blue-black serapes; but neither appeared in the least bothered by the bitter-cold mists which wreathed the trees and paths like wraiths and parted only before the chill winds which now and again blew gustily down from the snowy mountains behind them.

The group did not always take the best-known and most-worn paths, those which followed at an easy slope to avoid difficulties of the terrain; but frequently they availed themselves of shortcuts of the most precipitous kind. Yet not so much as a pebble was dislodged, and all difficulties vanished before their feet as though magically smoothed away.

By and by the intense cold grew less and the descent of the land less abrupt. They halted. The Indians consulted among themselves a moment. Then old Tuc turned to the towering figure of the Elder Old One.

"Lord, here we can take one of two paths," he

said. "This, to the left, is unavoidably longer than
this, to the right. But the one to the right connects
with the old road from Ixta, and—"

"And there the evil Huitzili-things are encamped.
I understand. It would be well to avoid them. They
have often defeated us. They may defeat us again. It
is possible. It is possible that we may defeat them. Or
we may miss them or they miss us altogether. Indeed, all things are possible, except that none may
miss Time and none may hope to defeat Him.

"Therefore: the path to the right."

In a moment all had passed: torch, censer, Indians, aliens. Nothing remained to mark their passage but a fallen and trampled leaf and on the still,
chill air the fragrant smell of copal-gum.

The Huitzilopochtli paused, lowered its monstrous
head. Behind him . . . well behind him . . . one of
its men-priests said, "Dragon-Head, Drinker of
Blood, the path to Moxtomí-town and thence to Popo
lies in the other direction. Pardon your slave: pardon,
pardon—"

"It is neither the town as a place nor the mountain
as a place which concerns us," the Huitzili said,
subduing its terrible voice to a muted murmur. "We
are concerned with the creatures called the Great Old
Ones: principally concerned with them: and I smell
that they have passed along this way and that they
have turned down that way. More: many men have
passed with them, and their bodies contain beating
hearts and their bodies contain the essence of life,
which is blood . . . which is blood. . . ."

The voice died away to a drone, the fearful head wagged as it turned. Its fellows droned their understanding and their acceptance, they turned, too. And the men-priests and the women, too, understood, turned . . . shivered with more than the cold wind and the freezing mists and icy dews . . . shivered with anticipation and exultation.

"*Blood . . .*"

"*Blood . . .*"

They turned, swung about, followed the lead figure. Its monstrous snout, which only the monstrous imagination of the Aztecs could have likened to that of a hummingbird, swung from side to side, snuffing up the wind, gathering information from the lingering scents along earth and air. From time to time it muttered, ". . . *men* . . ." and from time to time it mumbled, ". . . *hearts* . . ." and from time to time it droned, ". . . *blood* . . . *blood* . . ."

Gorgeous in glittering embossment and plumage, hideous in masklike visage, the other Aztec "gods" went clinking and clattering, stumbling-dancing, swaying-stamping, flapping-prancing, bawling and braying reduced to a minimum— stopped abruptly as the chief Huitzili-thing stopped in front where it had been smelling as it ran, like a dog.

"Other men were here," it grunted, half-pleased, half-annoyed. "Three other men. . . . All paused a while but not a great while. . . . Odd. No anger. I smell no anger. Different men, quite different, but no anger between them. How perverted. Enough!" The great head swung up once more. "Onward and after them! For we seek the Puissant Object called the Great Heart of Tlaloc and it may be that they will lead us to it, after which, if so, we will accept their hearts and drink their blood and nourish our needs. But let us be wary of both entrapments and willful resistance, never forgetting how perversion engenders a disposition towards both.''

In another moment all had passed in the darkness, leaving behind a trampled leaf and an odor of rotting blood, of hatred hot as fire, of stale sweats engendered by alien suns and ancient lusts, and of hungers long unappeased by never so loathsome feasts under never so distant moons.

Far away, far down the valley, a dog sleeping behind a heap of corn raised its muzzle and widened its nostrils. For a moment it stayed quite rigid. Then it shivered violently, a deep growl muted in its chest; and then it lifted its head and it howled.

Luis moved as fast as any of them, but he heard scarcely a word which was said. His eyes were glazed with bliss and his face wore an expression of frozen joy. A song sang in his heart and in his head, and its words were of the true old gods, the veritable angels, the return of the proper patron saints of the Moxtomí-Toltec-Olmec peoples, older than either the god or angels or saints of Mexican Christendom. Its words were of the terribly long delayed, but now about to be realized, return of the great days, with all things to be as they were, not only before the Spanish conquest but before the Aztec conquest as well. Sometimes his words passed his lips and sometimes they did not, but he was scarcely aware of this, either.

The Elder Old One said, "You are called Roberto?"

"Yes, Your Reverence," Macauley answered, feeling more than a little confused, but desiring very much to be polite, at all events.

"What is that, Roberto, which you have with you?"

Ahead, tight, tiny, the few lights of Los Remedios had begun to gleam an uncertain welcome in the black velvet fabric of the night.

"Why, it's called *dynamite*, Your Honor. . . . I used to be a miner, that's to say—but I guess you know. Anyway, more or less out of habit, I generally have some on hand in case of who-knows-what. These are sticks of dynamite, these are detonation caps, fuses—" He explained the uses and applications as they proceeded on towards the town.

The Elder Old One nodded. "Crude, but effective in a limited way. We will hope its use will not be necessary. Perceive: that light which appears to be burning in the middle of the air: it is on top of the hill now called Monte Sagrado?"

Macauley nodded. "Yes. . . . And the entrance I suggest is on the other side of the hill. For that reason as well as the obvious one of secrecy, I suggest that we go around the town instead of trying to go through it." He took out a Cuautla *puro* and lit it and let a mouthful of smoke billow out.

He had scarcely taken a second puff when a dog howled somewhere off in the distance and one of the Moxtomí gave a fearful exclamation. They halted, on one leg, so to speak, turned behind them without

precisely knowing why. The wind veered about and
struck them in the face and they recoiled. "The
Huitzili! They are following us!" a Moxtomí cried,
as the telltale air brought its message.

Macauley grunted. "Come on, then," he said.
"Double-time!"

The ground along the rough semi-circle which
they had to cover in turning the town was broken up
by fields and gulleys, hills and hummocks, the
narrow-gage railroad tracks of both the main line and
the spurs. It was not smooth going. Once they had to
veer to avoid the unfinished walls of the bullring, and
once Jacob slid and would have fallen into the gaping
foundation of a grain elevator if Macauley had not
caught him. Already behind them they could hear the
thumpthump-thumpthump of the pursuing feet, and
the not-quite-describable sound of voices, both
human and quasi-human, allowing excitement and
fury to unbridle the restraints of caution.

The troops of the first Montezuma had passed this
way, doing a deadly work of execution with those
war clubs inset with small blades of obsidian along
the sides. Cortez had passed on the same path, with
mounted men in armor upon armored horses, the
Indians, at first and for long, assuming the two to be
one creature, like a centaur. The swarming rebel
forces of patriot-priest Morelos; the gaudily uni-
formed cavalry of the supreme military mountebank,
His Serene Highness General Santa Anna; the red-
bloomered zouaves of the French Foreign Legion;
the shabby but deadly determined Constitutionalist
troops of President Juarez; the beautifully tailored,

efficiently tyrannical *rurales* of President Diaz;
every conceivable kind and type of revolutionary
band and army—all had come this way and gone this
way, and the town had been in its place and remained
in its place, had sometimes watched and sometimes
(in the person of its people) fled and sometimes
resisted and sometimes surrendered—

But never had the hills and fields observed any
stranger sight than they did now, and yet the town
stayed still and silent, the town slumbered and the
town slept.

Always those who mounted the wide and shallow
steps leading up around the *Monte Sagrado* had
mounted slowly and gravely and in reverence . . .
but not now. No one climbed slowly and painfully
and penitentially upon hands and knees, no one
paused to genuflect before the Stations of the Cross,
not a hair was torn out nor a garment rent to supply an
offering to the *ahuehuete* trees. The steps were
leaped by twos and threes and then the formal steps
were left behind and the running feet raced along a
tiny dirt path. A time-stained picture behind cracked
glass showed the painting of the Virgin of Guadalupe, as painted miraculously upon the mantle of
Juan Diego, in the fitful light of the tiniest of lamps
. . . the niche was beside a door ancient and massive of wood, reinforced with wrought-iron and
locked with an enormous and elaborate lock to which
there was no key.

Jacob Clay had ceased to think anything much
except, *What in God's name am I* doing *here? and
why don't I just stop running and go* home, *for*

God's sake? He watched, dumbly, numbly, as they
all came to a halt before the great gate sunken below
the level of the worn stone threshold. The giant who
(he was dimly aware) was known as the Elder Old
One, with no sign of haste or strain, put his fingers to
the lock and turned them as though they held a key.
He heard the key, the nonexistent key, he heard it
turn the protesting mechanism of the lock, heard the
click-clack-clock, saw the door swing open upon
loud-lamenting hinges. They entered. The door was
swung shut and locked again. Echo, echo,
echo. . . .

Probably few of the multitudes had, throughout
the course of pagan and Christian and secular centuries, been even dimly cognizant that the so-
seeming solid bulk of the Sacred Mountain concealed within it a sort of maze or labyrinth, hall after
hall, cave after cave, catacombs and chambers and
vaults. Old statuary in rich dim gilt leaned against the
rough-hewn walls, hands in stiff benediction raised.
Grills barred ways to neat heaps of monkish bones.
The splendid embroidered palls covering the Holy
Hermit next engaged their eyes in the gorgeous
gloom, but little dispelled by the huge dripping candles of brown beeswax on iron stands before the
cracked catafalque.

"Guardian, arise!" The Great Old One as he spoke
strode forward and touched the head and hands, the
only visible parts. The dark and sunken eyelids rose
and the candles glittered upon the dull eyes. The
hands moved, groped, found those of the Great Old

One, the covers were lifted and set aside, the figure which Luis had seen move before, moved now.

The Hermit set his feet upon the stone-flagged floors and moved, trancelike, down the dark and mazy corridors; the footsteps glowed and glimmered briefly before vanishing; they followed, followed, followed. Down winding passages, down flights of deep-cut steps.

Above, far above, muffled but audible, something crashed and battered at something. Something gave way. Monstrous feet trampled.

Door opened after door, door after door was closed. And the last door of all revealed a passage in the rock, a cleft—

"We cannot pass through," the Elder Old One said. The Guardian, seeming to awake more from its trance, spoke briefly. The noise from above increased. Jacob never afterward was clear as to what was said, he recalled the Great Old Ones departing along the level to an unknown destination, recalled slipping, squeezing, getting through the orifice in the rock, recalled wet and darkness and then a kindled torch and resinous smoke and flaring, spurting light and the great stone head in the falling spray and the old Moxtomí swinging his one-piece censer before murmuring chanting prayers through the clouds of odorous smoke. Smoke which increased the dimness. Heard the increasing clamor behind him, recognized the chanting and the hooting . . . braying . . . blaring . . . the combination of human and inhuman voices he had encountered in the woods the

night of the procession, a century or two ago—
—all happening very quickly—
—stones falling from the wall of the cave—
—the Great Old Ones thrusting their way through
the new-made opening—
—the Elder Old One standing beside the great
carven head with the enigmatic smile, something in
his hands which glittered and shimmered and
moved. *"Tlaloc, Tlaloc, Tlaloc-Tlamacazqui. . . ."*
Did the great carven eyes move? Did the great carven
lips tremble? What hideous sounds of clamor and
rage behind them! "Tlaloc, Tlaloc, Tlaloc-Tlamacazqui, give us your Puissant Heart. . . ." And
something moved, for certain and for sure, something came swimming through the surface of the
stone, something not unlike the thing held against the
stone by the hands of the Elder Old One, a something
which also glittered and shimmered and moved. The
two met, the two became one, then as deliberately
and inexplicably as before, something retreated back
into the stone as a stone sinks into ice, but swiftly.
And the Elder Old One, that which he held in his
hands now increased in size and light and weight,
walked. . . slowly. . . slowly. . . walked away.

But not very far away.

He turned, a look of regret briefly resting upon his
majestic and massive face, before giving way once
more to its expression of infinite calm. He turned, he
gestured. Jacob, Mac, Luis, the Moxtomí, found
themselves having gathered behind him. Saw the
other Great Old Ones moving forward with deliberate speed so as to form a shielding semi-circle around

their Elder. And saw, too, and heard, too (and felt, up through the floor—and smelled, as well—) the rushing onslaught of those who had pursued them.

Hideous muzzles stretched forward, inhuman eyes flashing redly, the Huitzili surged in upon them. And their allies from the debased Tenocha of the *Barrio Occidental* followed behind. Noise shouted and roared and echoed. It echoed still another endless second as all action ceased.

Then Huitzilopochtli spoke. "The Heart of Tlaloc!" it said.

Silence. A calmly resisting, a speaking silence.

"Old Ones, the Heart of Tlaloc! Let us have it, and you may then depart."

From his guarded position, the Elder spoke. "You may not have it. You may not have it because it is not yours. You may not have it because you would misuse it. It is not for you to say we may depart and it is not for you to say that we may not."

No shout followed on this, but from the gathered enemy came a low, guttering growl which was more chilling than any clamoring noise. Then the voice of Huitzilopochtli spoke up, low and intense and hideously grinding and echoing within itself. "Old Ones, our patience is short. Do not further abuse it. It is ours, the Heart of Tlaloc, because we defeated you before it was placed here. Surrender it and depart! Surrender it and flee once more to enjoy that peace which your perverted natures crave! Refuse, and we will destroy you forever. Now! At once! Relinquish the Object!"

The figures of the Great Old Ones did not move.

But from them a Voice composed of all their voices said, "If we are to be destroyed, we will not alone be destroyed. Better for us all here to perish here than for us to escape and leave you with the means of making millions perish."

Warm and golden, like the tolling of great golden-bronze bells, was that Voice, yet Jacob felt himself shivering faintly. The enemy spoke no word. The Great Old Ones spoke no word. The confrontation, delayed such endless centuries, was now upon them all. Jacob tried to still his shivering; he could not. It became a quiver, then a tremble. The coldness of fear and the fear of death, he thought . . . so it was like this. The coldness of fear and the fear of death. The coldness of death, now and here, before he was already dead. He compressed his lips, but a soundless sigh escaped him anyway, and he saw his breath smoke and vapor on the still, chill air.

It took a moment for him to realize what this meant, and what it meant made no sense. It was no chill that lay only within himself, arising from his own human fears and weaknesses. The cold he had been feeling was from outside. And it was not, and it could not have been, affecting him alone. He saw that Macauley's breath, and Luis's too, was visible . . . and, slowly, slowly, at first like a mere haze upon the air, those of the Great Old Ones as well. Their metabolisms were different, then. That was to be expected. Less water-vapor in their lungs? He dismissed the fruitless speculation. He wondered if some sudden cold front of the sort which American television meteorologists were always announcing as "coming down from Canada" had come all the way this far down.

Something disturbed his ear. A noise? A sound? He cast his eyes around. The great Head of Tlaloc sparkled and shone and it glittered with an icy mantle. Ice! No wonder he was so cold! So terribly, terribly cold. . . . It was not sound but the absence of sound which had disturbed him: the soft sound of seeping water falling like a spray of rain upon the Head of Tlaloc below the spring. Jacob saw the newly formed stalactites. Icicles. It was unnatural. Uncanny. Frost was now appearing on the walls, spreading like a leprous white fungus. The air cut his nostrils, he breathed through his mouth, his throat and lungs hurt, he thrust his hands between his legs.

Listen, stranger: snow and ice, and it grew wondrous cold. . . . He moved his icy-burning feet and heard the rime crackling beneath him.

He heard Luis draw in his breath, followed his glance, all but shrieked at what he saw. There, motionless as a frieze across the cavern, the Huitzili stood, burning red as fire. Heat rippled the air where they were, and he saw sweat rolling down the faces of the men and women beside them . . . among them he recognized Lupita, but he deliberately put this aside: he would wonder about this later. . . . Heat. Heat. Heat. . . .

It was evident what was happening. They were locked in silent struggle, a battle raging nonetheless on the level, perhaps, of the flux of subatomic particles. The Huitzili, deliberately, were sucking the warmth and heat from the air of the cave and from the

still-living bodies of their enemies, drawing the
warmth and the heat as a magnet draws iron fil-
ings, drawing it unto themselves and into themselves. . . .

Suddenly, almost shockingly suddenly, three
things happened: the cold fled, the warmth returned;
the Elder Old One had thrust his hand into the Heart
of Tlaloc . . . one hand . . . the other he placed
upon the shoulder of the Old One next to him . . .
who extended his hand to another . . . who did the
same . . . it was Luis's hand which lay so warmly
upon Jacob's. . . . Warmth from the glowing engine called the Heart of Tlaloc. Thus, two of the
things: and simultaneously and horribly, the Huitzili
began the *Noise*.

It could not have come from their mouths and
throats and lungs alone, it was too great, too dreadful. Sound upon sound, wave upon wave, and Jacob
sobbed and fell on his knees and pressed his hands
over his ears. But still the Noise clamored and
echoed and rang and every cell in his body seemed
stricken with a deadly vertigo and he screamed and
screamed and—

"This must be the last for now," the Great Old
One said, his voice coming pained and painfully
through the sudden silence. Something like a waver-
ing shield, transparent but not utterly clear, had
fallen (or risen) between the two groups. "We must
begin to leave now, seek time—I do not yet know
how long we may have—" The other group beat
upon the rippling panel, assailed and assaulted and
were held back by it. "This must be the last for now.

We cannot, we do not dare continue using the Heart of Tlaloc this way." He went on to speak, but Jacob was no longer intent on listening.

He was watching Macauley, he was listening to Macauley. "I'm not sure about the amount of the charge," Macauley was saying, preparing his dynamite and thrusting it deep into an opening in the cavern. "I don't want to bring the whole mountain down on top of us, if I can help it—" He grunted. His hands moved. They seemed, to Jacob, to be moving slowly. But he said nothing, realizing that of this he knew as near to nothing as made no difference.

Again the voice of the Great Old One broke in upon his mind's ear. "—if I can somehow fix this barrier to remain a while, then it may be that we can destroy their ship. They will still be dangerous, but less dangerous; if they emerge from here—"

Mac said, companionably, puffing his cigar as though they were seated at ease over a bottle of gin, "Now, there's the matter of the fuse, too. Overlong, I may blow up an empty cave. Over-short, I may blow up a corridor full of . . . well . . . *me!* And, of course, you. Read much Kipling? His politics left much to be desired"—another grunt. He cut the fuse.—"but he could turn a neat phrase. *The widow-maker.* Always liked that one. . . . Okay. The fire goes," he gestured, *"here—"*

And then the Great Old One made a sound they had never heard from him before. Slowly, slowly, he began to withdraw the hand from within the alien engine called the Heart of Tlaloc. They all began to retreat. The shield, the barrier, rippled violently.

But not so violently as the beating of Jacob's heart as he began to move.

That moment, however bewildering, however confusing, had yet had some element of clarity. Confusion worse confounded succeeded it. The barrier gave way in one place . . . in another. . . . Hideous muzzles thrust forward. Knives. Struggle. Stench. Mac falling. Jacob seizing him, somehow grasping and pulling. Screams. Smoke. Luis, calmly bending to pick up the still burning cigar which had fallen from Macauley's lips. Crush. Trampling, dragging, dreadful noise, concussion, falling rock. Above, the stars.

X

From the hills above Los Remedios, the town and
countryside, the Monte Sagrado itself, all looked the
same. Slowly the mists rolled away, slowly the sun
came toiling up from behind the two mighty mountains, slowly the morning cookfires sent their thin
wreaths of smoke upward to be slowly dissolved
upon the winds. Heaps of big brown adobe bricks
stood curing in the air, cattle lowed and slowly
moved along the roads towards pasture. Burros
laden down with firewood passed them on their way.
A thin and melancholy scream announced an eagle in
the air. A thin and melancholy scream announced the
mas o menos coiling its way up along the narrow
tracks towards town. The bells of the three churches
broke into voice as they had each morning for hundreds of years, the great wheels turning, the bells
revolving, falling, falling back, the tongues resound-
ing against the sides, the sextons bending to the
ropes, rising, releasing, grasping, bending. The old

women in black picking their way along the unpaved
streets, the middle-aged women setting up their
breakfast stalls in the market. And from every house,
the sound, immemorial, older than the bells, older
than any sound of human kind except the sleepy
human voices themselves, the sound of the pat-pat-
pat of women's hands shaping the dough for the
tortillas.

"Where now?"

The Great Old Ones lifted their great hands.
"Some of us to our own vessel, hidden in Popo.
Some of us to the vessel of the Huitzili-things, hidden in the crags of Ixta. We will destroy it. And
thence, we hope, barring Time and Chance and the
Unforeseen—things which no one and nothing can
bar—thence to our own world."

The Indians, listening, burst into tears. *"Viejos
Poderosos,* do not leave us! Stay with us and restore
the days of old, for we have waited for them as we
have waited for you!"

The smile of the Elder Old•One was something
less than, something more than, melancholy. Something akin to, something other than: "No one and
nothing, younger brothers, can restore the days of
old. Can one restore the melted snows? Can the bird
return to the egg? And yet, younger brothers, new
snows will fall, much like the old; and new birds will
hatch from new eggs. Think no more, or at least
think not much, of the days of old which may
have been good. Think instead of the new days to
come which may be good." The Elder Old One

gestured. Another of his kind moved forward, holding in his arms a great chest. He set it down and regarded, first it, then the weeping and now beginning to murmur Moxtomí with gentle wonder not unmixed with mild pleasure. "Here is something which we had almost forgotten, for it is not a thing we value. *The sweat of the sun, the tears of the moon.* What are they called in more modern words?"

Old Santiago Tuc, tears still wet upon his face, but even more than a mystic disappointed, a hunter and a farmer and a man more familiar with facts than with dreams; Santiago Tuc looked up with quickening excitement and said, "Gold? Silver?"

"Some silver. More gold. Yes. . . . The years which were years of lost labor because of your lost lands, younger brothers, ah . . . gone forever. But the land remains, the earth abides. Take it, then, tokens that we are not false altogether. It will regain the lost lands for you, and one will hope that new years and good years will grow therefrom for you."

Macauley and Clay shook their heads when asked about Luis's family. He had had no hopes in that family; that family had had no hopes in him. All of his hopes had been with the Moxtomí, and in their now-realizable hopes of reclaiming through purchase the lost Moxtomí communal, *ejido*, lands, the Moxtomí were fulfilling all of his dreams which were worthy of fulfillment.

Mac said, "I didn't even think he was listening when I explained about the dynamite. I didn't even think he was paying attention when the balloon started going up, down there inside of the *Monte*. But he had been and he was, sure enough. . . ."

Jacob Clay winced, nodded. "It didn't occur to *me*. Not to do what he did, not even to realize what he was doing when he was doing it." But the memory of the young man came back strongly and clearly as he spoke: Luis, face no longer blissful and enchanted, but a strong and totally calm male face. Luis bending to pick up Macauley's still lit, still burning *puro*, waiting until all the others—Great Old Ones, Moxtomí, and Jacob (with the help of young Deuh) carrying Macauley—had gotten out of the cave, then himself moving with deliberate haste and lighting the fuses from the cigar and tossing the sticks of dynamite—one against the opening through which most had entered, one against the larger opening the Old Ones had made for themselves—then moving purposefully against the third opening, the doorway of escape, and standing there with the burning charge in his hand so that none others might pass.

Until it, too, had gone off.

Side by side the two Americans walked down towards the town. "We might have asked them for, oh, I don't know—some sort of a souvenir, maybe," Macauley said. "What do you think? Hey?"

Jacob didn't think so. "No one would believe us, anyway," he said. "Unless we turned up with that whatever-it-was that they had. That machine or engine or . . ." He waved his hand, at a loss for words. "And from what they tell us about that, the sooner it gets lost, the better."

A passing herd-boy paused a moment as he came up to them.

"Did you feel the *temblor*, Señors?" he asked.

"What *temblor*, young one?"

"Ah, you did not feel it, then. During the night, Señores, a *temblor* in the town. It cracked several of the steps upon the Monte Sagrado, and overthrew that old archway on the edge of the town. Other than that, no damage—" He broke off to lope after his cattle.

Macauley grunted. "As I understand it, though, after the exchange . . . or the transformation . . . whatever you want to call it—*you* saw it! Damn it! Did those things slide between the subatomic particles coming in and out and back again, or *what?* Hell. . . . But anyway, it's my impression from what they were telling us that neither remaining . . . what's the word I want? 'Device,' there . . . that neither remaining device is harmful.

"Oh, well. You're probably right, though. Nobody would believe us. Unless maybe the Saucer Cultists, and I guess we can do without that. . . . What do you suppose the devices are good for, now?"

Jacob shrugged. "Making rain, maybe," he said. They both laughed.

Neither could resist going back to the Monte Sagrado and joining the crowd which stood and examined the cracked steps. "Securely, it was nothing more than a minor earthquake, such as has happened time after time here in the Valley," someone was saying; (Jacob recognized him—the merchant

Lopez, member of the Constitutional *Ayuntamiento* of the town) "possibly because of the proximity of *los volcanes.*"

But not everyone agreed with him. And one old man, so agitated that he removed his enormous old-style sombrero and struck it with his hand, cried, "And I tell you, Don Procopio, that, securely, it is nothing of the sort! It is the work of *el Tlaloc!* A warning that he is not to be molested—"

Don Procopio Lopez scoffed. "Do you call yourself a Christian?" he demanded.

The old man wagged his head. "I do, I do, and I tell you what every child knows: that *el Tlaloc* is himself a Christian, converted, *probablemente,* by the blessed Apostle Señor Thomas himself when *el santo* visited Mexico after the death of Our Lord—as witness that the emblem of the Tlaloc is a cross." The crowd murmured. "Can anyone deny this?" the old man demanded.

A market woman, of those who knelt hour after hour, usually, alongside a pile of produce, without visible show of weariness, now nodded her head vigorously.

"*Mira,* Don Procopio, he has reason, this old one," she said, emphatically. "The Tlaloc is very well where he is. It is said that he is himself a quality of saint—the saint of rain. How is it otherwise that the Holy Hermit made his home above the Tlaloc? Have the priests been molested by our Tlaloc? Has the bishop? No! Why then should the government and the military molest him?"

Don Procopio began to perspire very slightly. On the one hand, he was a member of the government and obliged to defend its doings; on the other hand, he was a businessman, and his customers were right here in the crowd and not among *los burocráticos* in the Federal District. "You also have reason, Señora Veronica," he declared. "I can assure you that is not the motive of our institutional and revolutionary government to molest el Señor Tlaloc, no, no—on the contrary—it is nothing more than the intention, without embargo, to remove him from his present obscure position in which he faces danger of destruction by earthquake and thus to bestow him with the utmost respect to a position of equal honor and greater salubrity—"

Macauley tugged at Jacob's sleeve and muttered in his ear, "Let's get on up and see what's doing." Jacob nodded. They gently slid through the crowd, which was already beginning to evince a degree of persuasion.

"The time is past," they heard Don Procopio orating, "when our national treasures and patrimonial heritages can be suffered to molder in the darkness. Does not the work of the Revolution still continue? Are not new schools, new centers of health and maternal care—"

Macauley murmured that he would not be surprised if Don Procopio did not eventually rise to the position of Alternate Member of the Chamber of Deputies, or something equally commensurate with his talents. "He's wasting them peddling galvanized nails here in Los Remedios—hello! *Soldados.*"

Sure enough, the entire cavalry troop seemed to be engaged on something quite important on and inside of the Monte Sagrado—not, to be sure, on horseback, though. There was much running back and forth, excited shoutings, and—as a sort of double-take—their way was barred by an armed guard. "Damn," Mac said, low-voiced. "Look—picks, shovels, pit-props. . . . They're going to excavate! I suppose that we might have known that they'd excavate! We should have realized! The *militario* was sent here to secure the Tlaloc . . . and they are damned well going to *secure* the Tlaloc! . . . or know the reason why. Damn, damn, damn."

The guard continued to face them with a sort of this-is-merely-me-in-my-official-capacity attitude, without menace or resentment. *Orders, Señores, are orders,* his face said . . . *another time, and you can buy me a drink . . . but just don't come any further or I shall be obligated to fusillade you.*

Jacob said, "I just thought of something. You suppose there's anything *left* of the Tlaloc?"

His friend sighed and shrugged and winced. *"I just thought of something. You suppose there could be anything still *alive* in there?"*

"Ugg. Christ. Yes, I mean, I hope *no*. You mean—"

"I mean." They faced each other. "Of course, there aren't—weren't—many of them. . . ."

"Who knows how they reproduce? Or what they might do? Just suppose that any of them are alive and

say just enough to alert, say, the Air Force, to recon-
noiter around the tops of Popo and Ixta before the
Good Guys take off . . . ?''

There was then, in the indeterminate distance, a
muffled scream. A shout. Many shouts. Another, or
perhaps the same, scream. Less muffled. Growing
louder. Feet running, trampling, stumbling. Voice
shouting. The guard moved warily so that he was
able to cover with his weapon both the two foreigners
and what until that second had been his rear. And
another soldier came into sight, face insane with
fear. *"¿Joven, que pasa?"* the guard cried.

*"Ah—ah—ah—not masks—not masks—no
hearts—no hearts!"* the fleeing one screamed and
babbled. *"Ai, Jesusmaria, men whose hearts were
torn out!—things of nightmares—ai!—ai!"* He
clawed at his eyes, staggered, slumped to the ground
in a faint.

"I guess that there *was* something still alive in
there," said Macauley, looking rather sick.

Jacob swallowed. "And I guess we can guess
what they've been up—" He stopped abruptly. His
eyes, Mac's eyes, the eyes of the guard, all swung
around to the opened gate which led into the depths
of the Sacred Mountain. The sound was ragged and
prolonged. It was repeated. And again. Jacob said,
"Three volleys. . . ."

The guard had begun to tremble. "Oh, my
mother," he muttered. "What has this poor one
seen? What are they shooting at in there?"

They never knew if he ever found an answer. Very

shortly a file of soldiers appeared at port arms, eyes staring and mouths sagging; at their head, their commanding officer. ". . . don't know and don't want to know," he was saying in a high, tight voice only kept by great self-control from being a shout. "Wall them up, what's left, forever, and—". He stopped short on seeing the two foreigners.

Macauley asked, crisply respectful, "Are all dead, colonel?"

"Securely, they are all dead, and pray God they all remain so!" Something seemed to click behind the eyes of *Coronel* Benito Alvarez Diaz. He drew himself up. "I do not know exactly or even approximately what you may think you may be referring to, Sir Macauley," he said. "But this I *can* assure you: the United Mexican States constitute a secular, a totally secular Republic; and as an educated man and a freemason I not only do not fear, I indeed totally defy all superstition, whether Christian or pagan!"

His eyes blazed at them. Macauley made a gesture in between a salute and a bow. "I understand, Colonel, and I respect infinitely both your motives and the compliment of your confidence."

"It's well. . . . Now, for the love of God, get out of here, say nothing, and let us all have a good, stiff drink!"

It was quite a good while later before Jacob got back to his own patio, walking with exaggerated care, and smelling strongly of *Oso Negro* gin. He found Sarah in so deep a mood of self-sorrow that she barely bothered to scream, "Where have you been all night, you son-of-a-bitch?" at him, as he, breathing heavily, pulled off his shoes with all four hands and needing every one of them, too.

"Dispense, dispense," he muttered. "Work of utmost importance to peace and happiness of future generations. Elder gods. Bad guys. Smelled real bad. Foreign names. Can't pronounce. Don't get wrong idea," he cautioned, crawling onto the bed. "Some are all right. Best friends. But not in same neighborhood."

Sarah began to weep. It was all too much. Not alone that he had been gone all night and now had come home stinking drunk. But Lupita, evil and wicked and faithless Lupita, had yet again and yet once more failed to show up. And so once more and yet again she, lovable and put-upon Sarah, was left with a pile of dirty dishes and greasy pots and nothing to wash them in, or with, but ice-cold water. "You bastard," she sobbed. "A lot you care!"

From halfway along the bed Jacob opened one bloodshot eye. "Let one in," he cautioned, "first thing you know: brings in his whole family." He closed his eye, was instantly and catatonically unconscious, and began to snore like a demented lumber mill.

Señora Mariana, the landlady, and her sister, Señora Josefa, were properly sympathetic. "Ah, the poor pretty norteamericaness!" they sighed to her. "Yes, yes, we have sent to inquire, and the response is that la Lupita is not encountered at all today; no, no, Señora, she is not to be found. What barbarity!''

"But why?" Sarah demanded. "Where can she have *gone?*"

They shrugged. They shook their heads. "Thus it is, Señora. One takes the troubles to teach these girls the proper management of a household, and as soon as they have learned, what passes? Always, but always, Señora, they go off to 'Mexico,' where they can make more pesos. Thus it is today, Señora, but it was not thus when we were young. You are well off without that cruel Lupita. Very well off,'' they nodded, seriously.

Sarah thought that they might well be right. But . . . still. . . . What was she going to *do?* How would she manage, up here so high that water scarcely boiled, no O-cello sponge mops, no Campbell's soups, no Comet cleanser, no detergents— and now: no maid?

They did not entirely understand her, but they were sympathetic nevertheless. "Do not weep, poor pretty Señora," they urged. "All men become drunk, but observe in how much more civilized a manner become drunk los norteamericanos! And as for a girl, *pues*, Señora, have no concern: my sister and I will inquire, we will seek, we will securely find you another girl to aid you.''

Sarah smiled a wobbly but already-begun-to-be-reassured smile. "You *will?*"

"Oh, without doubt, Señora!"

"Absolutely, Señora!"

"Oh, good! That's all right, then. . . . *When?*"
"Mañana, Señora!"
"Mañana!"

Partly as a result of the eloquence of Don Procopio in pointing out that active noncooperation might well result in peril to the basic Revolutionary principals of Effective Universal Suffrage and No Reelection of Presidents, and partly as a result of rumors that Colonel Alvarez Diaz had already shot a large number of resisters and interred their bodies up within the Monte Sagrado, further resistance to the removal of Tlaloc melted like snow in the summer sunshine.

Further troops arrived, archaeologists arrived, engineers arrived, gigantic machinery of all sorts arrived, a special railroad spur was constructed; and so, little by little, and with infinite pains, the Tlaloc was slowly removed through a new-made opening in the side of Monte Sagrado, gently eased down the slope, hoisted aboard the flatcar, and conveyed and convoyed by day and by night slowly and carefully the entire length of the *mas o menos* line to its terminus in the ancient Estacion San Lazaro in the City of Mexico. Here it was placed with equally painstaking care onto the specially constructed, specially reinforced bed of the most powerful truck in the Federal District: and, slowly, slowly, slowly, under constant military and civil escort, conveyed along its route to its new home in the new Museum of National Antiquities and Patrimonial Treasures.

Tlaloc's fame had gone before him, as such things have a way of doing. By the time the truck was underway it was well past midnight. Nevertheless, the route, which passed by a total of twenty-seven churches and the cathedral, was lined with what traffic experts calculated must be at least two million of the five million inhabitants of the City of Mexico. As the truck bearing the gigantic stone head, its eyes half-closed, on its full lips an expression of infinite majesty and calm, passed on its slow way through the throng, not a sound was heard.

Not a sound, that is, except the continual sound of the pouring down of what all observers and all records agreed was by far the heaviest cloudburst of rain ever seen on that date in any year in the entire Valley of Mexico.